LOVE,

Jerry Spinelli

LOVE, STARGIRL

Alfred A. Knopf

New York

THIS IS A BORZOI BOOK PUBLISHED BY ALFRED A. KNOPF

www.randomhouse.com/teens

Educators and librarians, for a variety of teaching tools, visit us at
www.randomhouse.com/teachers

Library of Congress Cataloging-in-Publication Data
Spinelli, Jerry.
Love, Stargirl / Jerry Spinelli. — 1st ed.
p. cm.
SUMMARY: Still moping months after being dumped by her Arizona
boyfriend Leo, Stargirl, a home-schooled free spirit, writes "the
world's longest letter" to Leo, describing her new life.
ISBN 978-0-375-81375-7 (trade) — ISBN 978-0-375-91375-4 (lib. bdg.)
[1. Love—Fiction. 2. Eccentrics and eccentricities—Fiction. 3. Home schooling—Fiction.
4. Diaries—Fiction. 5. Letters—Fiction. 6. Pennsylvania—Fiction.] I. Title.
PZ7.S75663Ls 2007
[Fic]—dc22
2007002308

Printed in the United States of America
August 2007
10 9 8 7 6 5 4 3 2 1
First Edition

Starlight contains many colors. My heartfelt thanks to Donna Jo Napoli; Will Marinell; Jim Nechas; Patty Gauch; Kathleen Lindop; Rosemary Cappello; Molly Thompson; Ellyn Martin; Anthony Cappello; Pat Strawn; Tom Reeves; Kathy James; Katie Carmichael; Joan Donaldson; Sean James; my cousin Patty Maud for her medical counsel; Alvina Ling for lending me her name; my editor, Joan Slattery, who lent me time away from Anna and Grace; and my wife, Eileen, for lending me her life.

As of this writing we have sixteen grandchildren.
To each of them this book is dedicated:

Amanda

Will

Jill

Ashley

Dan

Ryan

Zachary

Courtney

Rachel

Natalie

Michael

Sarah

Kathy

Leah

Angel

Lana

LOVE,

January 1

Dear Leo,

I love beginnings. If I were in charge of calendars, every day would be January 1.

And what better way to celebrate this New Year's Day than to begin writing a letter to my once (and future?) boyfriend.

I found something today. Something special. The thing is, it's been right in front of me ever since we moved here last year, but today is the first time I really saw it. It's a field. A plain old vacant field. No house in view except a little white stucco bungalow off to the right. It's a mile out of town, a one-minute bike ride from my house. It's on a hill—the flat top of a hill shaped like an upside-down frying pan. It used to be a pick-your-own-strawberries patch, but now it grows only weeds and rocks.

The field is on the other side of Route 113, which is where my street (Rapps Dam Road) dead-ends. I've biked past this field a hundred times, but for some reason today I stopped. I looked at it. I parked my bike and walked into it. The winter weeds were scraggly and matted down, like my hair in the morning. The frozen ground was cloddy and rock-hard. The sky was gray. I walked to the center and just stood there.

And stood.

How can I explain it? Alone, on the top of that hill, in the middle of that "empty" field (Ha!—write this down,

Leo: *nothing* is empty), I felt as if the universe radiated from me, as if I were standing on the X that marked the center of the cosmos. Until then I had done my daily meditation in many different places in and around town, but never here. Now I did. I sat down. I barely noticed the cold ground. I held my hands on my thighs, palms up to the world. I closed my eyes and dissolved out of myself. I now call it washing my mind.

The next thing I noticed was a golden tinge beyond my eyelids. I opened my eyes. The sun was seeping through the clouds. It was setting over the treetops in the west. I closed my eyes again and let the gold wash over me.

Night was coming on when I got up. As I headed for my bike, I knew I had found an enchanted place.

January 3

Oh, Leo, I'm sad. I'm crying. I used to cry a lot when I was little. If I stepped on a bug I'd burst into tears. Funny thing—I was so busy crying for everything else, I never cried for myself. Now I cry for me.

For you.

For us.

And now I'm smiling through my tears. Remember the first time I saw you? In the lunchroom? I was walking toward your table. Your eyes—that's what almost stopped me in my tracks. They boggled. I think it wasn't just the sight of me— long frontier dress, ukulele sticking out of my sunflower shoulder sack—it was something else too. It was terror. You knew what was coming. You knew I was going to sing to someone, and you were terrified it might be you. You quick looked away, and I breezed on by and didn't stop until I found Alan Ferko and sang "Happy Birthday" to him. But I felt your eyes on me the whole time, Leo. Oh yes! Every second. And with every note I sang to Alan Ferko I thought: *Someday I'm going to sing to that boy with the terrified eyes.* I never did sing to you, Leo, not really. You, of all people. It's my biggest regret. . . . Now, see, I'm sad again.

January 10

As I said last week, I wash my mind all over the place. Since the idea—and ideal—is to erase myself from wherever and whenever I am, I think I should not allow myself to become too attached to any one location, not even Enchanted Hill, as I call it now, or to any particular time of day or night.

So that's why this morning I was riding my bike in search of a new place to meditate. Cinnamon was hitching a ride in my pocket. As I rode past a cemetery a splash of brightness caught my eye. It was a man sitting in a chair in front of a gravestone. At least I think it was a man, he was so bundled up against the cold. The bright splash was the red and yellow plaid scarf he wore around his neck. He seemed to be talking.

Before long I found myself back near my house, in a park

called Bemus. I climbed onto a picnic table and got into my meditation position. (OK, back up . . . I'm homeschooling again. Gee, I wonder why—my Mica High School experience went so well! Ha ha. So I have to meet all the state requirements, right?—math, English, etc. Which I do. But I don't stop there. I have other courses too. Unofficial ones. Like Principles of Swooning. Life Under Rocks. Beginner's Whistling. Elves. We call it our shadow curriculum. ((Don't tell the State of—oops, almost told you what state I'm living in.)) My favorite shadow subject is Elements of Nothingness. That's where the mind wash comes in. Totally wiping myself out. Erasing myself. (((Remember the lesson I gave you in the desert?))) Which, when you think about it, is really not nothing. I mean, when I'm really doing it right, getting myself totally erased, I'm the opposite of nothing— I'm everything. I'm everything but myself. I've evaporated like water vapor into the universe. I am no longer Stargirl. I am tree. Wind. Earth.)

OK, sorry for the detour (and parenthetical overkill). . . . So there I was, sitting cross-legged on the picnic table, eyes closed, washing my mind (and getting school credit for it!), and suddenly I felt something on my eyelid. *Probably a bug,* I thought, and promptly washed away the thought, and the something on my eyelid just became part of everything else. But then the something moved. It traced across my eyelid and went down my nose and around the outline of my lips.

Then a voice, woman's, harsh: *"Dootsie!"*

Then: "Hello. My name is Dootsie. I'm a human bean. What are you doing?"

I opened my eyes. A little girl was sitting cross-legged in front of me. A lady was hurrying toward us, appearing stricken, saying, "I'm *so* sorry. My daughter gets away from me sometimes. I'm *really* sorry."

"It's OK," I said. I was groggy, like waking up. I looked at the little girl. Dootsie. "I was meditating. I was being nothing."

Dootsie frowned. The sun brought rusty highlights to her curly hair. She reached out and touched me again. She laughed. "You're not nothing." She poked my knee. "You're right there."

"To me I was nothing," I said. "It's hard to talk about."

She frowned again. Suddenly her mouth and eyes shot open. "You pretended!"

I nodded. "Sort of."

She studied me. "Are you a magician?"

"Nope."

She beamed. "I'm a magician!"

"Really?"

"Aren't I, Mommy?"

"A regular Houdini."

Dootsie climbed down from the table. "I can make myself disappear. Watch."

She squeezed her eyes shut. She whispered something I couldn't make out. She stood at attention and turned around three times. She whispered again. A slow-moving grin came over her little round face.

I looked around. "Where are you?"

She giggled. "I'm right here. You can hear me but you can't see me."

I swished my hands in front of me. "Hello? . . . Hello? . . . Dootsie? . . . Are you there?"

Dootsie's eyes goggled. She whispered, "Mommy . . . she doesn't even *hear* me!"

Her mother winked at me. "Dootsie . . . say something to the nice girl so she'll know you're there."

Suddenly Dootsie's eyes double-goggled and she shrieked, "A mouse!" and came leaping at me, very visibly. Cinnamon must have wondered what all the talking was about. He had poked his head out of my coat pocket, and before I knew it, he was cradled in the little girl's hands.

"Actually, he's not a mouse," I told her. "He's a rat."

She rubbed her cheek against his cinnamon fur.

"Put your nose up to his," I said.

She did. Cinnamon's tiny tongue came out and kissed her on the tip of her nose. She squealed.

While Dootsie was nuzzling Cinnamon, her mother held out her hand. "I'm Laura Pringle."

We shook. "Stargirl Caraway."

Dootsie gaped. "*Stargirl?* That's your *name?*"

"Sure is."

"You're new in town?" said Mrs. Pringle.

"Since last summer," I said. "We live right over there"—I pointed—"Rapps Dam Road."

"Not the house with the brown shutters, by any chance?"

"Exactly."

She smiled, nodded. "My brother. Dootsie's uncle Fred and aunt Claire. They used to live there. Dootsie knows your house as well as her own."

Dootsie held out Cinnamon. She whined, "Mom-*mee* . . . she has a rat and the best name and she sits on tables. I want to be her!"

Cinnamon was getting fidgety. I took him back. "Hey, I was just thinking I want to be *you*. I mean—'Dootsie'? Names don't come any cooler than that. Plus, you can make yourself disappear. You are *so* cool. Do you take a cool pill every morning?"

She looked at me all serious. She shook her head. "No."

"So I guess you're just naturally cool, huh?"

She nodded. "I guess."

"Tell you what," I said. "I've never been cool, and I've always wanted to be. So how about we trade places? You be Stargirl and I'll be Dootsie."

Her eyes rolled up to the trees. Her finger pressed her bottom lip. "Not yet," she said. "I want to be Dootsie some more." She thought again. "Till I'm ten."

"Okay," I said, "when you're ten we'll switch."

"Okay."

We shook on it. Then Mrs. Pringle said it was time to leave me in peace, and off they went, Dootsie whining, "I want a rat!"

January 15

I take field trips. Hey, who doesn't? Who says I'm not a normal student? In fact, I take lots of field trips. My mother sends me to a small area in town where my assignment is to hang out for the day and then write a poem about my experience there. I might stay for ten minutes or ten hours—however long it takes me to come up with a poem. I take my notebook and do the poem right there.

Today was a real challenge. The destination was "the stone piles." (My mother slips a card under my bedroom door with the field trip location.) She meant the old abandoned cement plant. There's the rickety dull green skeleton of the building and some rusting equipment and three piles of stones about as tall as me. They used to be much higher, I hear. People keep taking the stones for their gardens and stuff, and kids throw them. Well, here's how it went:

FIELD TRIP:
FOREVER AT THE STONE PILES
How long have I been here?
Not a clock in sight. What the heck—call it forever.
The stone piles and me.

It's one thing to walk past
a pile of stones.
It's another to sit with one
forever.
Do that and you begin to
learn about things you thought
you knew,
like silence
stillness
smithereens.
And now
(can forever have a now?)
I hear something—footsteps—
no not steps—
gravelsliding shlurping—
footshlurps—
and here he comes—
navy peacoat, moss-green knit
pullover cap with perky pom-pom moss-green tassel,
slow, slumpy—
if he were a Snow White dwarf
he would be Droopy—
round, puffy, whiskered face—
donut dough with gray and black whiskers—
shuffling, drooping toward me,
sees me—or does he?—
there's a stone pile silence and stillness
in his eyes—

says, croaks, "Are you looking for me?"—
shuffles on by, doesn't wait for
an answer.
I want to call out, *Hey! . . . Wait!*
but he's moving on,
the back of him now
shuffling . . . shuffling . . . green pom-pom bobbing
    bobbing bobbing

January 16

Pounding on the front door woke me up. My clock said 6:15. I put on my robe, wobbled down the stairs. My father was long gone to work. My mother creaked from her doorway: "Who this early?"

I opened the door. For a half moment all I saw was the house across the street. Then I looked down. It was Dootsie. "Where's Cimmamum?"

I called back to my mother, "It's the little girl I told you about. Dootsie."

I brought her in. She wore pajamas under her coat. Her slippers were Miss Piggys.

"Where's Cimmamum?"

"Cinnamon's sleeping," I said. "Like you should be."

My mother came down, stared at the slippers. "Dootsie? Where are your parents?"

"Are you Stargirl's mommy?" said Dootsie.

"I am."

"Are you Starmommy?"

We laughed.

The doorbell rang. It was Mrs. Pringle, eyes wild. "I'm *so* sorry. Dootsie's gone. Did she—" Then, looking past me: "Dootsie! Thank God!" She scooped up her daughter and breathlessly told us she had been listening to talk about Cinnamon for days, and when she found the empty bed this morning, the first place she thought of was her brother Fred's old house.

Dootsie reached out and tugged on my mother's sleeve. "I want pancakes."

Five minutes later Mrs. Pringle, Dootsie, Cinnamon, and I were at the dining room table while my mother mixed pancake batter in the kitchen.

"She's getting worse," Mrs. Pringle was telling us.

"I'm getting worse," said Dootsie. She was playing with Cinnamon, standing him up by his paws and making him dance.

"It started with climbing out of her playpen," said Mrs. Pringle. "Then getting lost at the mall. At the beach." She shuddered at a memory. "Now"—she looked at her daughter, wagged her head, smiled four parts love, one part exasperation—"she's learned how to unlock the front door."

"Does she cry when she gets lost?" I said.

"Never."

"So she doesn't think she's lost."

"Far as she's concerned, she's never been lost in her

life. And there's nothing she can't do. She thinks she's thirty-five."

Dootsie was in her own world. She lifted Cinnamon's feet off the table and let him swing. "Whee!" She twitched her nose against his. She giggled as he climbed to her shoulder and nosed into her ear, then sat on her head. Suddenly she yelped, "Wait! Let me!" She bolted for the oven as Cinnamon flew into my lap. My mother held her at the skillet while she poured batter onto the sputtering griddle.

Mrs. Pringle looked at the ceiling. "Help!"

January 19

My happy wagon is almost empty, Leo. Only five pebbles left. Happywise, I'm operating on only 25 percent capacity. Remember when I first showed my wagon to you? How many pebbles were in it then? Seventeen? And then I put another in, remember? I never told you this, but before I went to bed that night, after we kissed for the first time on the sidewalk outside my house, I put in the last two pebbles. Twenty. Total happiness. For the first time ever. It stayed that way until I painted that big sign on a sheet and hung it outside the school for all the world to see . . .

STARGIRL
LOVES
LEO

Was that my mistake, Leo? Did I overdo it? Did I scare you off? It seems like ever since then I've been taking pebbles out of the wagon. And now it's down to five and I feel rotten and I don't know how to feel better.

So I played hooky today. My mother trusts me to play hooky every now and then. (In fact, we have a course called Hooky, but not for credit.) I just got on my bike and rode. Rode and rode. Now that I think of it, I was heading west. To Arizona? Somewhere along the way I heard a sound. I looked up. A Canada goose was flying across the gray sky. Honking. I've never seen a solo goose before. They always fly in V-shaped flocks, or at least in pairs. Had he been left behind? Was he trying to catch up, calling, "Hey, wait for me!"? Had he just lost his girlfriend and was calling out her name? Was she dead? Or flown off to Arizona with another goose? One voice honking across the sky. The loneliest sound I have ever heard.

And then I thought of the bundled man in the cemetery. I turned back. I hadn't realized I'd come so far from town. I rode to the graveyard. There he was, same spot, sitting in an aluminum folding chair, green and white strapping. This time I went in. His chin was on his chest. He was dozing. Most of his face was lost behind the brilliant red and yellow plaid scarf. An old-fashioned black domed lunch box sat in the grass under the chair.

I was afraid to go too close. I foot-pushed my bike around behind him. There were two names on the gravestone: Grace and Charles. Under her name were the dates of her life. Under his name were his birth date and year, then a dash, then nothing. Death day to come. Under that was TOGETHER FOREVER.

Grace. It was her second date that surprised me—she died four years ago. And still he was here. Grace. I think she gave him the scarf. I think she called him Charlie. *Grace.* I whispered her name.

I backed away as quietly as I could.

January 27

I babysat Dootsie today. Her mother and father said they needed to "escape."

Dootsie lives on Ringgold Street, a short bike ride away—but a long walk for a little girl on a cold day at six in the morning. I still can't believe she did that. When I arrived she was invisible. You know she's disappeared when you see her standing at stiff attention with her face scrunched and her eyes squeezed shut. She was in a corner in the dining room. I said to her mother, "Well, it looks like Dootsie's gone. Nobody here for me to babysit. I guess Cinnamon and I will have to go home. Bye."

As I turned to go, Dootsie screamed. "No! I'm here! I'm here! I'm just imizible!" She came running. "Cimmamum!"

So I stayed and the Pringles went out and Dootsie played with Cinnamon and then we painted her room. She paints her room almost every day. She's allowed to paint anything she wants in her room except the windows. Walls. Doors. Furniture. Think: balloon filled with 50 paint colors bursts and splatters room. Think: squashed aliens. Think: little-kid paradise. Don't think: little-princess room with canopy bed and ruffles and frills and pink. So there I was, brush in hand, letting loose the bedroom-painting maniac that hides in all of us.

Then we talked about you.

Dootsie: "Do you have a boyfriend?"

Me: "I'm not sure. I used to."

Dootsie: "What's his name?"

Me: "Leo."

Dootsie: "Is Leo a human bean?"

Me: "We're all human beans."

Dootsie: "Do you love him?"

Me: "I think so."

Dootsie: "Does he love you?"

Me: "He did. And then he didn't. I think he will again."

Dootsie: "When?"

Me: "Someday."

Dootsie: "Where is he?"

Me: "In the state of Arizona. Far away."

Dootsie: "Why?"

Me: "Why what?"

Dootsie: "Why is he far away?"

Me: "He goes to school there. I moved here to Pennsylvania." (Oops . . . now you know. We moved to your home state. Well, I won't narrow it down any more than that.)

Dootsie: "Did he kiss you?"

Me: "Yes."

Dootsie: "Did he kiss Cimmamum?"

Me: "Yes."

Dootsie: "I don't wanna talk about him anymore."

So we talked about other stuff and painted some more, and then she said, "Let's go visit Betty Lou."

"Who's Betty Lou?" I said.

"Our neighbor. She's afraid to go out. She's diborced."

This sounded interesting. I left a note on the dining room table in case the Pringles came home early, and we went next door and rang the bell. The door seemed to open by itself. No one was there, but a voice said, "Come in."

"She's behind the door," Dootsie said, and waltzed in. She waved. "Come on."

I went in, the door closed, and standing before me was a person in a purple bathrobe and bright red slipper socks. Dootsie pointed at me. "This is my friend Stargirl. She kissed a boy named Leo."

The person shook my hand, smiled. "Betty Lou Fern." Dootsie thrust out her hand, which Betty Lou shook also. "Did she tell you I'm afraid to go out?"

"Right after she told me you're the neighbor."

She laughed. A big, bold laugh. "She tells everybody. The whole town knows I'm agoraphobic. Isn't it silly?" She waved us on. "Come into the kitchen. I'll make us hot—EEYOWWW!"

Suddenly Betty Lou was standing on a dining room chair, screaming, "A rat!"

Cinnamon was poking his head out of Dootsie's coat pocket.

"It's just Cimmamum," said Dootsie. She pulled Cinnamon out and offered him to Betty Lou. Betty Lou screamed louder.

I took Cinnamon. "Cinnamon is my pet rat." I lowered him deep into my pocket. "He's really tame and friendly."

"But he's a *rrrat*." She snarled the word. "There's a *rrrat* in my house." She stepped up onto the table. The teased top of her black and gray hair was flattened against the ceiling. She was trembling.

"I'm really sorry," I said. "We'd better go."

"No!" shrieked Dootsie. She jabbed her finger. She scowled. "Betty Lou, you come down here. *Right now.*"

"I can't."

And then a new look of horror came over Betty Lou. She covered her eyes with her hands. "Stop!"

I looked at Dootsie. She had rolled her eyeballs up till they disappeared. Mucho creepy. "Are you coming down?" she said.

Betty Lou squeaked, "Are you going to keep the beast out of sight?"

"Yes."

"Are you going to let its tail touch me?"

"No."

"Put your eyes back."

"Okay." Dootsie's eyeballs rolled back down into place. "I did."

Betty Lou came down and made hot chocolate. She took donuts out of the freezer and warmed them in the micro-wave. "I always have something good to eat for Dootsie. That's how I lure her over here. Since I'm afraid to go out, I have to find ways to make people visit me."

Dootsie piped, "I'm her best visitor!"

Betty Lou laughed. "She's right. She visits me almost every day."

"And every day I get a donut!"

Betty Lou nodded. "Once a week I have a dozen deliv-ered from Margie's Donuts."

She took a bite of her crème-filled. "Mmm. Margie calls them the best in the world. She's right."

I asked her, "Do many people have agoraphobia?"

"More than you might think." She glanced nervously at the living room. I had taken off my winter coat and put it on the front porch. Cinnamon was warm in the pocket. "Don't rodents flatten themselves?" she said. "Do you suppose he could squeeze under the front door?"

"He can't make himself that flat," I told her. "You're safe."

"The word 'agoraphobia' comes from the Greek," she said.

"It means fear of the supermarket!" piped Dootsie.

Betty Lou laughed. She curled her fingers in Dootsie's hair. "Close enough. When she hears me say it a few more times she'll get it right. It's fear of the marketplace. And

Dr. Dootsie's personal diagnosis for me *is*—" She nodded at Dootsie.

"She's a mess!"

Betty Lou howled. For someone so fearful, she seemed surprisingly jolly. "It just popped out of her mouth one day: 'You're a mess!' I haven't stopped laughing yet."

"So it's not just the marketplace you're afraid of," I said.

"It's everywhere." She pointed. "Everywhere on the other side of that door. Isn't it silly? I keep telling myself, *There's nothing to be afraid of.* Look at all those other people walking around out there—all those human beans, as Dootsie would say. Nothing bad is happening to them. But I can't seem to convince myself."

I tried to imagine being afraid to go outside. I couldn't.

"How long?" I said.

"Nine years now," she said. "It started on a beautiful sunny day in May. May nineteenth. The birds were singing, the flowers were blooming, the weather was warm. It was one of those perfect days you get a couple times a year. I had my garden gloves on because I was going to the backyard to plant my tomatoes. I had three tomato plants in those little green plastic boxes. Better Boys. And I went to open the back door and the knob was stuck. I couldn't seem to turn it. I tried and tried, even with two hands. Finally it turned, but by then—I don't know—it's like something had happened, like that stuck doorknob was telling me maybe I didn't want to go out after all. And then the phone rang, so I took off my gloves and went to answer it. It was my old friend Hildegard. We always talk forever. When I finally got off the phone, there were two messages waiting, so I dealt with them, and then it was time to make lunch and then I had to watch my soaps, and it wasn't until the next morning that I noticed the three tomato plants still on the kitchen counter. And somewhere deep inside myself I knew I didn't really want to . . ."

She stopped. She stared at the counter, but she was seeing something farther away. I don't think Dootsie and I were breathing.

". . . want to . . . plant them anymore," she went on. "So I just stood at that back door there"—she nodded to it— "and just stood there and stood there and stared at the doorknob, and finally I quick reached for it and turned it and suddenly the door was open, and I just . . . stood there. I couldn't move. The fresh air washing over me felt threatening. The world outside that . . . that rectangular door frame, it was all too much, too big. Dangerous. I'd like to tell you I fought valiantly with myself, that I tried really hard to step over the threshold into the backyard. But I didn't fight. I knew I wasn't going to do it. I closed the door and I haven't opened it since. I only open the front door to let in visitors."

"She doesn't even put her hand out to the letter box!" said Dootsie.

"Not even that," said Betty Lou. "Dootsie brings my mail in. She stands on a porch chair and reaches in and gets it. I have my groceries delivered."

Dootsie blurted: "And donuts!"

"And donuts," said Betty Lou. "A girl named Alvina brings them from Margie's every Monday."

Dootsie frowned. "I hate Alvina."

Betty Lou frowned. "Be nice."

"Alvina is a grump."

Betty Lou laughed. "True. But Alvina brings your donuts, doesn't she? She leaves them on the porch and Dootsie brings them in with the mail."

"Wow," I said. "Quite a system."

Betty Lou nodded. She smiled sadly. "Wow is right. It's called coping. And I haven't even told Dootsie this yet— the other day for about ten seconds I was almost afraid to come out of my bedroom." She looked around the room. "Good grief. Afraid of my own house. I'm getting worse."

"Hey!" piped Dootsie. "I'm getting worse too. Mommy said."

"And did Dootsie tell you I'm divorced?" said Betty Lou.

"I'm afraid so."

"She calls her old hubband Potato Nose!"

"Mr. Potato Nose," corrected Betty Lou.

That gave us all a laugh. We did a lot of laughing until Mr. Pringle came to the door to fetch Dootsie. As I rode my bike home, I kept thinking of two people—the lady in the house who won't go out and the man at the cemetery who won't go in.

February 6

Snow.

Gobs of it. Up to my knees. Up to Dootsie's ears. We made a snowman. I took Cinnamon out of my pocket so he could see it. I put him on my shoulder. I sneezed. The sneeze knocked him off. We looked down. Nothing but a hole in the snow. Cinnamon! Four hands digging frantically. We got him. He was freezing. Shivering. His tail was blue. We breathed our warm breaths on him and rubbed him and kissed him. When he kissed us back, we knew he was going to be OK, even though his tiny tongue was cold.

February 14

Leo Loves Stargirl
☐ yes
☐ no

February 18

Do you know what day this is, Leo? It's First Kiss Day. Four days after Valentine's. One year ago tonight. Outside my house. My happy wagon was full. I was so stuffed with happiness there wasn't room for any more.

Today I took one out. It's down to four.

February 22

Field trip assignment: Margie's.

Margie's little donut shop. It's on Bridge Street between Pizza Dee-Lite and Four Winds Travel. The sign says BEST DONUTS IN THE WORLD!

I went for lunch. I had a powdered-chocolate and an old-fashioned. There are four counter seats and one small table. I sat at the table and watched the customers come and go. Margie said she didn't mind, she was glad for the company. Margie is plump, like her crème-filleds, an explosion of bleached blond hair. She's a talker. She talked to everybody who came in. She never stopped talking to me. By 2:00 p.m. I knew that she lets her underarm hair grow in the winter, that beans don't give her gas but chickpeas do, and that the most glorious thing in her life is getting her feet rubbed.

I was surprised how many people eat donuts for lunch. The four counter seats were always occupied. Margie is taking donuts where no donuts have gone before. You want chicken soup for lunch? Fine, open a can. But you want *donut* soup? It's Margie's or nowhere. She's also got donut pudding and a donutwich, and she says a donut pie is "in development."

I had already started to write my poem, called "Donut Soup," when I heard a loud thump and the door blew open and suddenly there was a girl in the middle of the shop, squatting, panting, facing the door, screaming red-faced at three boys on the sidewalk:

"Ya ya ya ya ya!"

The boys yelled back:

"Yer ugly!"

"Yer dead meat!"

"Everybody hates you!"

Margie came flapping her arms. "Scram!" The boys scrammed.

Turns out the girl works there. Not officially. She's too young. Eleven. Gets paid in donuts. She comes in after school. Sweeps, dusts, washes, bags trash, bothers Sam the donut maker in back.

She came sweeping toward me. She stopped, stared. "Ain't you eating?"

"Not at the moment," I said.

"So you gotta go," she said. "You can't just sit here. Bums do that. You gotta buy something. This is a business. It ain't the Salvation Army."

"I'm not a bum," I said.

"So buy something."

So I bought another powdered-chocolate, just to keep the peace.

She went off sweeping but came back in a minute. "What are you writing?"

"A poem," I told her.

"What about?"

"Donuts," I said. "Or maybe you."

She sneered. "Yeah, right." Her short weedy hair looked like something Cinnamon would be happy nesting in. She wore a blue and red striped T-shirt and a yellow plastic Pooh Bear on a black shoestring necklace. "What's your name?"

"Stargirl."

She gaped. "*Stargirl?* What kind of name is that?"

"I gave it to myself," I said.

She sneered. "You can't name yourself."

"I did." She stared at me, blinking. The broom was still. "So what's your name?" I said.

"I hate my name."

"I won't."

"Alvina."

"That's cool," I said. "It's different. Old-fashioned."

"Yeah, like a donut."

"Alvina . . . ," I said, remembering. "Are you the girl who delivers Betty Lou Fern's donuts each week?"

She glared. "What if I am? You got a problem?"

I put up my hands. "Hey, just asking."

She pointed at my notebook. "That poem really about me?"

"Could be," I said. "Not sure yet. I'm waiting to find out if you're interesting or not." I gave her a tilted squint. "Are you?"

"I'm boring."

I laughed. "Nobody's boring."

"I stink."

I laughed again. I took her arm and sniffed it. "You smell okay to me."

"I'm ugly."

"No you're not. Don't listen to those boys."

"I hate boys." She picked up the broom and held it like a machine gun. She stepped back. She sneered and raked the shop with her jittering broomstick-and-bullet chatter. "I'd kill them all. I'd line them up and mow 'em down. Every one. Thousands. Millions!"

"That's a lot of ammo," I said.

"I hate 'em," she said, and went back to sweeping the floor.

I doodled poem lines for a while. I looked up to find I was the only one in the shop. Everyone else was in back. Then . . .

FIELD TRIP:
STOMPING AT MARGIE'S
The door opens slowly.
The boys come in, quiet,
sneaky, grinning.

They look at me, eyes asking,
Will you spoil it?
My eyes reply, *I'm the poet.*
I'm writing this. You're
living it.
One puts finger to lips: *Shhh.*
I change my mind: "No!"
Too late—
fast as boys, they're behind
the counter, scooping donuts, armloads,
squealing boy squeals,
Margie rushing in—"Hey! *Hey!*"—
the boys rushing out, donuts spilling—
one boy at the door stops, turns, drops
a raspberry-filled to the floor, raises his knee
to his chest, yells "Yee-hah!" stomps,
the donut squirting raspberry all the way
to the counter.

"Don't try to save them," says Margie.
"Throw them away."
Alvina sweeps the fallen donuts with great care
into a heap.
She shapes, she molds the heap
with her broom.
She looks at the boys mocking
in the street, laughing,
gorging, spewing donuts.

The broom clatters to the floor.
She jumps,
both feet come down on the
pile of donuts,
up down
up down
she stomps the donuts like she
used to stomp puddles when she was
little,
stomp
stomp
stomp
while the boys, frozen now,
gape, open mouths full of
unchewed donut.

February 28

It snowed yesterday. Today the world is white. I put on my boots and walked to Enchanted Hill. It was as pure and perfect as a new sheet of paper. I took one step onto the field and stopped.

What was I doing?

The pure whiteness, dazzling in the sun, was one of the most beautiful things I had ever seen. Who was I to spoil it? Snow falls. Earth says: *Here—a gift for you.* And what do we do? We shovel it. Blow it. Scrape it. Plow it. Get it out of our way. We push it to our fringes. Is there anything uglier or sadder than a ten-day-old snow dump? It's not even snow anymore. It's slush.

Was that beginning to be us, Leo? I'd rather never see you again than have that happen. We were once so fresh, a dazzling snowfield. Let's promise to each other that if we ever meet again we will never plow and push our new-fallen snow. We will not become slush. We will stay like this field and melt away together only in the sun's good time.

I backed off carefully, stepping out of the one footprint, and walked away.

March 3

I saw the first flower of the year today. A crocus, peeking out from under a bush, like, *Hello! I'm here!* A little purple dollop of cheer and hope. I cried. Last year at this time I was the crocus, popping out, blooming with love and happiness for you, for us.

To make matters worse, I was with Dootsie.

"Why are you crying?" she said.

I tried to smile. "Happy tears. First flower."

She studied me, all serious. She shook her head. "Bullpoopy."

In spite of myself, I almost burst out laughing. "Where did you get that from?"

"My father. He says it when I lie to him. I lie a lot."

"I'm not lying."

"Bullpoopy."

"Okay, I'm lying."

She studied me some more. Her eyes were watering. "It's your boyfriend, isn't it? He made you cry."

"No."

"Bullpoopy." She stomped on the ground. She was angry. "He dumped you."

I shook my head. I couldn't speak.

"Yes he did! He *dumped* you!" And her little face collapsed and she burrowed into me and clung to me.

When I got home I took another pebble out. Three now.

March 6

ARIZONA PEOPLE I MISS MOST

1. You

2. Archie

To you Archie is the old "bone hunter" who retired from teaching and came to Mica. He talks with his beloved cactus, Señor Saguaro, and he invites you and other kids to his back porch, where he smokes his pipe and leads your meetings of the Loyal Order of the Stone Bone. He's all that to me too—I still wear my fossil necklace—and he's much more. You know, my mother didn't recruit him to help her with my homeschooling. He volunteered. He's the one who came up with the original shadow curriculum. Nothing I learned from him helped me when the State of Arizona came testing. He gave me more questions than answers. He made me feel at home—not in his house or even in my own, but in the wide world. He is like a third parent to me.

3. Dori Dilson

Some of the kids at Mica High turned against me. Some turned away from me. Dori was the only one who did neither.

March 10

Every day brings a new memory of something we did a year ago. A parade of unhappy anniversaries.

March 11

I had a dream last night that I was meditating in Archie's backyard, under the outstretched arm of Señor Saguaro. Suddenly an elf owl flew out of the Señor's mouth, and he spoke to me: "Bullpoopy."

"Wait till I tell Archie what you said," I said.

"Bullpoopy on him too," the Señor said.

And then he spat at me. Something hit my cheek. It stung wickedly. I shrieked. I pulled it out. It was a cactus needle.

"That wasn't nice," I said.

"Ptoo!" He spat another needle. Pain in my neck. I pulled it out. And then they came and came: "Ptoo! Ptoo! Ptoo! Ptoo!" Prickly pain all over me, and every time I pulled one out, two more would hit, and they weren't cactus needles anymore, they were tiny darts, tiny darts with red feathers sticking all over me, and the faster I pulled them out, the faster they came, and I couldn't reach the ones in the middle of my back. . . .

I woke up sweating, tingling. I put on my sweatpants, coat. No shoes. I tiptoed downstairs, out of the house. I rode my bike to Enchanted Hill. I walked to the center. The ground was cold and clumpy against the soles of my bare feet. I liked the feel of it. The hard, real *now-ness* of it.

I felt alone on the planet, drifting through the cosmos. With both hands I reached out to the night. There was no answer. Or maybe I just couldn't hear it.

March 12

Dear Stargirl,

Hey, you're a big girl now. Stop being such a baby. You think you're the only one who's ever lost a boyfriend? Boyfriends are a dime a dozen. You want to talk loss, look at all the loss around you. How about the man in the red and yellow plaid scarf? He lost Grace. BELOVED WIFE. I'll bet they were married over 50 years. You barely had 50 *days* with Leo. And you have the gall to be sad in the same world as that man.

Betty Lou. She's lost the confidence to leave her house. Look at you. Have you ever stopped to appreciate the simple ability to open your front door and step outside?

And Alvina the floor sweeper—she hates herself, and it

seems she's got plenty of company. All she's losing is her childhood, her future, a worldful of people who will never be her friends. How would you like to trade places with her?

Oh yes, let's not forget the footshuffling guy at the stone piles. Moss-green pom-pom. What did he say to you? "Are you looking for me?" It seems like he hasn't lost much, has he? Only . . . HIMSELF!

Now look at you, sniveling like a baby over some immature kid in Arizona who didn't know what a prize he had, who tried to remake you into somebody else, who turned his back on you and left you to the wolves, who hijacked your heart and didn't even ask you to the Ocotillo Ball. What don't you understand about the message? Hel-loooo? Anybody home in there? You have your whole life ahead of you, and all you're doing is looking back. Grow up, girl. There are some things they don't teach you in homeschool.

> Your Birth Certificate Self,
> Susan Caraway

March 13

She's right, of course. Every word is true.

It's just not the whole truth. She doesn't mention how you looked at me in the lunchroom that first day. Or how you blushed when your best friend, Kevin, said, "Why him?" and I tweaked your earlobe and replied, "Because he's cute." Or how nice you were to my rat even though you were terrified. Or how proud you were of me when I won the speech contest in Phoenix. Or how—I don't know, how do you explain it?—how we just fit together.

OK, so you're not perfect. Who is?

Sure, Susan makes sense. But my heart doesn't care about sense. My heart never says: *Why?* Only: *Who?*

March 14

Today, for the second time, I rode into the cemetery. It was getting dark. The man Charlie wasn't there. I coasted along the winding pathways. Moonlight and tombstones. A vision came to me. I was in the graveyard of my own past. Under each tombstone lay a memory, a dead day. Here Lies the Day in the Enchanted Desert. Here Lies the Day We Followed the Lady at the Mall and Made Up Her Life. Here Lies the Day We First Touched Little Fingers, Stargirl and Leo's Secret Signal of Love.

Each night I lie down in a graveyard of memories. Moonlight spins a shroud about me.

March 15

My happy wagon is down to two pebbles.

March 16

I hate you!

March 17

I miss you!

March 18

I hate you!

March 19

I love you!

March 20

I hate you!

March 21

LEO!

March 22

Now see what you did. You made me miss the start of spring. It happened yesterday, but I was so busy moping over you that I didn't even notice. I'd probably still be in the dark if I hadn't gotten a letter from Archie today. He asked me if I saw the sunrise on March 21. Archie and I used to go into the desert and watch the sunrise on four special dates: the Vernal

Equinox (March 21), the Summer Solstice (June 21), the Autumnal Equinox (September 22), and the Winter Solstice (December 21). We poured green tea into plastic cups and toasted each new season.

Yesterday the sun was directly over the equator. Day passed night. Winter became spring. With every turn of the earth now, day is leaving night a few more minutes behind. The universe is going about its business. Why am I surprised?

March 23

All my father said last night was, "Go to bed early." I didn't ask why, but I knew. Sure enough, he woke me at 2 this morning, and 30 minutes later we were having grilled sticky buns and coffee at Ridgeview Diner. I knew what he was doing. He's noticed my mood. He was trying to perk me up. He believes that the answer to anyone's problem is to go on a milk run.

Confused?

Yes, my father is a milkman now. After fifteen years as an engineering supervisor at MicaTronics, he was burned out. Still, he wasn't going to quit. But my mother made him after she asked him what he would rather do and he grinned and said, "I always wanted to be a milkman."

So we loaded the truck at the warehouse and headed for the Friday route. As the truck turned a corner at a Wawa store, the headlights suddenly caught a face. It was a face in a Dumpster, wide-eyed with surprise. And then we were gone.

"See that?" said my father.

"I did," I said. I was still seeing the face, like the afterglow in my eyes when I turn away from the sun.

The Friday route is in the southern part of the county. Developments. Farms. Solitary homes along curvy country roads. No streetlights. No traffic. Only the dark and our own headlights and the rattle of glass bottles in the racks behind us.

The customers leave notes, Scotch-taped to the door or rolled and rubber-banded in the metal milk box on the front step. Some order the same thing every week, some different. Some parents let their kids write the note. Like:

> Dear Mr Milkman,
> Pleeze leave 1 gal skim
> 1 qt choc
> 2 cott cheese
> 1 doz eggs
> My cat Purrfecto loves your milk!!
> Love,
> Cory

I've gone on other Friday milk runs with my father, and there was one address I was especially looking forward to. It came early in the run: 214 White Horse Rd. The Huffelmeyers. The Huffelmeyers are an old couple. They get one quart of buttermilk, one quart of chocolate each week. But my father doesn't leave their stuff on the front step—he takes it inside. See, the Huffelmeyers remember the old days, when things were safer and they left the front door unlocked all the time and the milkman just came in and put their stuff in the fridge. And that's the way they keep it. At 214 White Horse Road it's still 1940. We just walk on in. Dad turns on a small table lamp with a fringed shade so we can see. We stay as quiet as we can. While Dad heads for the kitchen, I like to stop and look at the pictures. There must be a hundred family photographs in the living and dining rooms. I watch them go from black and white snapshots— the young married couple, he in his World War II uniform, she in a floral dress and wide-brimmed hat, standing arm in arm in front of a Ferris wheel—to color pictures of the old couple surrounded by kids and grandkids and, it looks like, great-grandkids.

Leo, some people might say it's creepy, tiptoeing through someone's house at four o'clock in the morning—but it's not. It's wonderful. It's a sharing. It's the Huffelmeyers saying to us, *Come into our house. Look at whatever you like. Get to know us. We're upstairs, sleeping. Feel free to stroll through our dreams and memories. We trust you. And don't forget to take the empty bottles.*

An hour later we left the weekly cottage cheese and orange juice in the kitchen of the Dents, who are even older than the Huffelmeyers. My father headed east then, toward a silver-gray sky. New day coming. So far we had hardly said a word to each other. Now we did, though the conversation was stop-and-go, shorthand, constantly interrupted by the rattle of the milk carrier as my father hustled off to another customer.

Dad: So.

Me: So.

Dad: Blue these days?

Me: More like gray.

Dad: I see you're down to two pebbles.

Me: You noticed.

Dad: Leo Borlock?

Me: Leo Borlock.

Dad: Still?

Me: Still.

Dad: Worth it?

Me: Not sure. I think so.

Dad (*his hand on mine*): One thing you *can* be sure of.

Me: That is?

Dad: Me.

Me (*smiling*): I know.

Dad: And Mom.

Me: I know.

By the time we headed home, kids were pouring onto the playgrounds of grade schools for morning recess.

March 24

I was pretty OK the rest of yesterday. Puttered around the house. Visited Betty Lou's with Dootsie. Then, as soon as I was alone—bedtime—it all came back.

I dreamed of Señor Saguaro again. This time he didn't spit darts. He didn't speak. I couldn't even see his mouth. Then I realized it was on the other side of him. I walked around to his back, and the mouth moved to the front. And that's how it went: wherever I looked, the mouth moved to the other side. Soon I was desperately running in circles around the old cactus, trying to catch up with the mouth, because I knew that only when I caught up to it would it speak to me.

I'm disappearing, Leo. Like Dootsie's trick, except this is real. Who are you if you lose your favorite person? Can you lose your favorite person without losing yourself? I reach for Stargirl and she's gone. I'm not me anymore.

I went to the stone piles today. I had a feeling that the shuffling man would come by again, and he did. Still wearing the moss-green knit pullover cap and tassel and navy peacoat, still gravelsliding along. He stopped in front of me. He said, "Are you looking for me?" and shuffled on without waiting for an answer. I called after him, "I'm looking for me! Have you seen me?!" but he just kept on moving, green tassel bobbing. . . .

March 27

I played homeschool hooky. I stayed in my room all day—writing, reading, daydreaming, remembering. My mother didn't object, didn't ask why. I wrote three haiku and two lists. Maybe I'll send you the haiku someday. Here's the first list:

THINGS I LIKE ABOUT LEO
1. You loved me
2. You liked my nose freckles
3. You were nice to my rat
4. You loved Archie
5. Your shy smile
6. You followed me into the desert
7. You held my hand in front of everybody
8. You chose Me over Them
9. You filled up my happy wagon

And the second list:

THINGS I DON'T LIKE ABOUT LEO
1. You dumped me
2. You liked Susan more than Stargirl
3. You weren't brave enough to be yourself
4. You chose Them over Me
5. You're emptying my happy wagon

March 29

Down to one pebble.

March 30

Leo! Save me from an empty wagon!

April 1

I had promised Dootsie I would take her to Bemus Park to-day. At the first corner we came to, Dootsie said, "I wanna wear them." She was pointing at my earrings, the little silver lunch trucks that my father had a silversmith make for me in Tucson. I took them off. I went to put them on her ears, but she said, "*I* wanna do it."

"Okay," I said, and handed them to her.

Next thing I knew she tossed them into the nearby sewer, threw up her hands, and cried out, "April fools!"

She was so pleased and proud of herself, I hated to spoil her fun. But you know me, Leo, I'm not exactly the world's greatest actress. I couldn't cover up my shock and disap-pointment. She saw it on my face. Her eyes grew wide, her smile vanished. She tugged on my finger. She peeped, "April fools?" I could only stare at the sewer grate. She howled, "I did it bad!" and started bawling.

I hugged her and calmed her down. How do you explain

the trickery of April Fools' Day to a five-year-old? I tried to tell her how it works. I told her that in the end, the important thing is that the victim feels relieved and happy because things aren't really so bad after all. The look on her face told me she wasn't getting it. But I would soon find out she was getting it all right—just in her own way.

We continued our walk to Bemus Park. Along the way I bought us each a pack of Skittles. It was the first warm Sunday of spring. The playground was an ant colony of little kids—swinging, climbing, darting this way and that, sawdust flying. Dootsie stationed herself at the bottom of the sliding board. As each slider landed, Dootsie held out a Skittle and said, "April fools!" Pretty soon every kid on the playground was lined up at the sliding board. When Dootsie's Skittles were gone, she took mine.

When the Skittles ran out, we started for home. We passed people in the park. Dootsie began unloading the rest of herself. To the first person, she gave a Mary Jane from her pocket. "April fools!" To another, she gave a pink quartz stone she had found. To another, a button that said THINK. To another, a paper clip. Each came with an "April fools!" and a giggle. And usually a puzzled smile from the recipient.

When her pockets were empty, she took the red plastic Cracker Jack ring off her finger and gave that away. Then the pink rubber band on her wrist. She panicked when she saw the next person coming and realized she was empty. She reached for my Stone Bone fossil necklace. "No!" I said.

I gave her the change in my pocket. Dootsie gave away my coins one at a time. I was hoping we would run out of people before we reached her house. We didn't. Dootsie gave away the last nickel and again went for the fossil necklace. I straightened up, keeping the necklace out of her reach. She kept jumping, reaching, squeaking, "Gimme! Gimme!"

I gave it. It was gone in a minute, and she was back at me. "Stargirl! More!"

"Dootsie," I said, "I'm empty. There's nothing left."

I was lying. There was one thing left. It was a tiny brown feather of an elf owl. I had seen it clinging to the bird's nest hole high in a saguaro near my enchanted place in the desert. I used a yucca stick to dislodge it. Since the day we moved from Arizona I've carried the elf owl feather everywhere I go.

Dootsie was going for my pockets. I blocked her. The feather had come to mean you. Us. Stargirl and Leo. Blocking my pockets only made her suspicious. She knew I was holding back. "You have something!" she wailed. She was crying. Crying for lack of something to give.

I had been crying a lot lately too. I remembered Archie's words, the words you told me he said to you once: "Star people do not shed tears, but light."

Dootsie was tugging. "Gimme!"

Give.

And what had that loose change been doing in my

pocket in the first place? Remember how it used to be, Leo? I never had change because as soon as I got some I would toss it onto the sidewalk to be found.

What happened to that Stargirl?

Shed.

Light.

Tears don't bounce. Light does.

I gave her the feather. She gave it to a man walking his dog. "April fools!"

April 2

And so I'm me again, Leo. Thanks to the example of a five-year-old. I'm hoping you wouldn't wish it any other way. Not that you weren't flattered, right? I mean, to have a girl two thousand miles away going to pieces over you, weeping at the mere memory of you, losing her appetite, losing her self and her self-respect—well, that's trophy enough for any guy's ego, huh?

You occupied my space. But because you were not in my present, when I looked into my future I saw . . . nothing. Isn't that sad? And stupid?

Well, I hope you enjoyed your smuggies while they lasted because it's over now. Oh sure, I'll still be missing you as much as ever. I'll still smile at the memory of you. I'll still be—OK, I'll say it again—loving you, but I won't abandon myself for you. I cannot be faithful to you without being faithful to myself. I've reclaimed my future. If we are destined to be together again, be happy to know you'll be getting the real me, not some blubbering half me.

So I gave my wagon a booster shot the other day—five pebbles! That's six now.

Spring has finally caught my attention. I say, "Good morning!" to daffodils.

And I'm dropping loose change again.

As for the paper money in my allowance, I have a new use for it. The local newspaper is called the *Morning Lenape*. (The Lenape tribe—it's pronounced *len-AH-pay*—used to live around here.) The paper has a section for classified ads. Three lines, three days, fourteen dollars. Most people use the section to advertise yard sales and such.

Here's my first ad. It will run Monday, Tuesday, and Wednesday next week:

**Dootsie Pringle
is the BEST April Fooler
in the world!**

April 11

Something happened today that was both disturbing and mysterious.

Dootsie has been sick with the flu, so I went over to let Cinnamon cheer her up. I had just left the Pringles' and climbed on my bike to head home when I heard a gruff voice behind me: "Hey."

It was Alvina. Charming Alvina. I stopped.

"Hi," I said. "Growl at anybody today?"

She ignored the question. "I'm going home from my job."

"I see," I said.

The little plastic Pooh Bear around her neck was holding out his arms and wearing a huge smile—unlike the sour face above him.

She threw a thumb toward Betty Lou's house. "That lady's getting wackier."

"Mrs. Fern?"

"Mrs. Wacko."

I asked her what happened.

"I left her donuts on the porch—"

"This is Wednesday," I said. "I thought you do that on Mondays."

She shot me a disgusted look. "If you stop interrupting me I'll tell you."

"Sorry," I said.

"So, yeah, I dropped them off on *Monday*. And they're always gone by the next day. Only yesterday—*Tuesday*"—she paused and glared, daring me to interrupt—"when I walked by, they were still there. And now today—*still* there."

Of course, I thought. *Dootsie couldn't take the donuts in because she's been sick. I should have done it myself. Stupid.*

Alvina went on: "So just now I rang the bell. The lady came to the door, but she wouldn't open it. I yelled at her, 'Open the door! I got your donuts!' Her voice comes back all squealy, 'I can't. I'm having a bad day.' I said, 'I'll give you a bad *week*,' but I don't know if she heard me." (I almost laughed.) " 'Can't you squeeze them under the door?' she squeals. 'Yeah,' I said, 'if I flatten them with a steamroller.' " (Now I *did* laugh.) "She—"

Alvina suddenly stopped talking. Her eyes darted over my shoulder. Her expression showed curiosity, then shock, then fury. "Hey!" she yelled past my ear, and practically knocked me down as she took off.

I turned to see, up the block, a boy on Betty Lou's porch. He had the white donut bag in his hand. He paused on the top step to look at us, then started running.

Alvina chased him up Ringgold, then into an alley where they both disappeared, though I could still hear her screaming. And then I couldn't. I had continued on my way home when she came puffing back down the street. She flung a finger toward Betty Lou's house. She yelled: "Serves ya right, ya *wacko*!"

She was close to me now, but suddenly she took five steps backward. She squinted. "What's *that*?"

I had taken Cinnamon out of my pocket and perched him on my shoulder.

"My pet rat," I said. "Cinnamon."

"You got a *rat* for a *pet*?" Her lip was curling as if she smelled something bad. Pooh Bear was still beaming.

"Best pet in the world," I said. "Come meet him."

She pointed, clearly at me, not Cinnamon. "You know what? You're wacko too." She crossed the street and continued on home, muttering, "This place is fulla wackos."

I detoured to Margie's and got some donuts and brought them back to Betty Lou's. I persuaded her to open the door enough to let me squeeze in. We had a nice talk, and we agreed that whenever she was having a bad day she would hang a red slipper sock in the front window, so Dootsie and I would be alert to give her special attention that day.

And all the time I was at Betty Lou's, I kept remembering the face of the boy on her porch. It was the same face I had seen during the milk run. In the Dumpster.

April 19

Sunrise.

It's been on my mind ever since the last milk run with my dad. Ever since Archie's letter. Ever since I turned back to the first page of this letter to you—which is becoming the Longest Letter in the History of the World—and read the first sentence.

And so I decided to wash my mind on Enchanted Hill one day a week—at sunrise.

My parents weren't too happy. They don't like my going out alone while it's still dark. On the other hand, they appreciate how attached I become to things like this. So we worked out a plan. We got walkie-talkies, one for me, one for my mother. And a flashlight for me. I'll do it on Thursdays. I started today.

My mother dragged herself out of bed and sat on the porch and watched me as I walked down Rapps Dam Road. She got stuck with the job because, of course, my father the milkman is long gone by then. With my flashlight on, my mother could see me almost all the way to Route 113. I crossed the road and a minute later I was in the middle of Enchanted Hill. The first thing I did was walkie-talkie my mother and tell her I was OK. It was still pretty dark out, but the sky was lightening by the minute. I sat on an old bath mat I carried along. I faced east and closed my eyes and dissolved into the elements. Sometime later, a glint in my eyes told me the sun was up and it was time to go.

When I returned home I expected to find my mother nodding off on the porch, but she wasn't. She was wide-awake. She smiled and hugged me and said, "Why do I have to be stuck with two people who leave the house in the middle of the night?" We laughed and went back to bed. Someday I hope I can be as good a mother as she is.

April 23

I want to leave a donut for the man at the cemetery—Grace's Charlie. But I'm a little shaky. Will I be intruding? Imagine that—Stargirl afraid of intruding!

April 24

OK—I decided. I'm going to do it. I bought a donut at Margie's. Cinnamon-sugar. I'll leave it at Grace's grave site tonight, so Charlie will find it tomorrow when he arrives. I'll be careful to put the bag beside the grave, not on top of it.

April 25

I chickened out.

April 26

I did it. (With a fresh donut.)

April 27

I went to the cemetery this afternoon. It was a warm, beautiful day. Balmy. He wore a gray sweater. The red and yellow plaid scarf was draped over the back of his chair.

I circled around behind him. I kept my distance. I didn't see the white bag. *He took it!* I thought, thrilled. Then I saw the bag, a few grave sites away. It didn't look like it had been opened. Lurched up against a tombstone, as if he had angrily flung it there. Maybe even kicked it.

I am a meddling, nosy, interfering, inconsiderate, intruding busybody.

April 30

I tried again.

May 1

Same story. This time he kicked it farther. Should I give up?

May 4

Dootsie and I touch little fingers—our secret sign of affection. Like you and I used to do. And I sadly think of what Archie says, that the sounds of extinct birds may be preserved in the songs of mockingbirds.

May 19

Dogwood Festival!

It's been going on since Monday, but today, Saturday, is the big day.

First the parade. People lining Main Street from downtown to Bemus Park. Bands. Fire engines. Dance academies. Little Leaguers. Clowns on unicycles. Politicians flinging candy from convertibles. The Dogwood Queen and her Court. The Grand Marshal was a TV weather lady.

Dootsie was all over the candy, a great white shark among guppies. Every time a three-year-old reached for a piece, Dootsie snatched it. She was stuffing them in her pockets, her mouth. When she stuck a mini Tootsie Roll up her nose, I drew the line. I yanked her out of the gutter, pulled the Tootsie Roll from her nose, squeezed her shoulders. "Dootsie, you're being a piggy and a bully. You're undoing all the nice things you did on April Fools' Day." She glared at me. She unwrapped a Mary Jane and popped it in her mouth. And spent the rest of the parade giving her candy away to three-year-olds.

Bemus Park was mobbed. Food stands sold everything from cotton candy and shish kebabs to funnel cakes and pierogies—and of course Margie's donuts. You could pitch pennies to win a goldfish or find your future in the fortune-teller's tent. There were rides for the little kids and a haunted house and open mike all day at the band shell.

Herds of teenagers roamed everywhere. I've never seen so many lip rings and purple hair spikes. To Dootsie it was a zoo. She kept tugging at me and whispering: "Look! . . . Look!"

At one point I happened to be looking at a food stand selling cotton candy and caramel apples when I saw the boy—the face in the Dumpster, the boy on Betty Lou's porch. Someone had just paid for something and the clerk had turned away to get change when the boy veered to the stand, reached out, plucked a caramel apple from the counter, and breezed on his way.

I started to pull Dootsie along after him—I don't know what I had in mind—but we didn't get far because just then

I heard a horrific shriek, and people were turning and running. Kid voices yelled, "Fight!" It was nearby, in front of the Rotary Club hot dog stand. Two kids were on the ground. The one on top was pummeling the one beneath, pounding fist on face. I was paralyzed. I can't remember ever seeing a real fight before. Until that moment, for me, one person striking another was something in books and movies. History. But history never made me queasy. All this happened in a few seconds, then two men were hauling the kids off the ground and pulling them apart even as they continued to flail at each other.

One was a boy, the one on the bottom. Blond. The other was Alvina. The boy's face was bloody from the nose down. There was even a streak of blood in his blond hair. I couldn't be sure, but he might have been one of the three boys at the donut shop that day. He was spluttering bloody noises at Alvina, who glared at him with a hatred I've never seen on a human face before, not even at Mica High last year. Then she made a fist and held it out to the boy and said in a soft snarl, almost a smile, teeth bared: "Taste this, punk." But something just before that had caught my eye. It must be new, because I'm sure I would have noticed it before. It was the nail on her little finger. It was different—not plain, not short, not kid-scruffy like the others. It was long. And pink. And glittery. It was elegant. And then it disappeared into the balled fist.

The men were pulling them off in opposite directions when Alvina screamed, "Wait!" She wrenched away from the man (mostly—he kept hold of her by one wrist) and went crabbing around on the ground until she found something. She picked it up, spat on it, cleaned it with her shirttail, and put it in her pocket. It was her yellow grinning Pooh Bear necklace.

In the next instant, one horror replaced another. I suddenly became aware of Dootsie's hand in mine. I looked down. She was looking up at me. Her lip was quivering. Tears streamed down her face. "Oh, Dootsie," I said. "I'm sorry." I snatched her up and ran.

I didn't slow down till I was out of Bemus Park. She was sobbing now, her little body heaving against mine. I tried to put her down, but she wouldn't let go of me. I walked some more, talking to her. "This was all my fault, Dootsie. Stargirl is bad. I never should have let you see that. I was only thinking of myself and I forgot all about my best friend Dootsie. I'll never forget about you again."

Her squeaky little voice came through the sobs. "Promise?"

I kissed her salty tears. "Triple promise."

Soon we were sitting side by side on the steps of the library.

"Alvina is mean," she said.

"She's a pip all right," I said.

"What's a pip?"

"Well, a pip is a feisty person. Someone who's maybe a little out of control."

"I hate Alvina."

I pulled her onto my lap. "No, don't hate Alvina."

"I *do*. I hate your boyfriend too. Because he *dumped* you."

I laughed. "Don't hate him either. You shouldn't hate anybody."

"I can't help it. I *have* to."

"No," I told her, "you don't have to. If you start by hating one or two people, you won't be able to stop. Pretty soon you'll hate a hundred people."

"A *zillion?*"

"Even a zillion. A little hatred goes a long, long way. It grows and grows. And it's hungry."

"Like Cimmamum?"

"Even hungrier. You keep feeding it more and more people, and the more it gets, the more it wants. It's never satisfied. And pretty soon it squeezes all the love out of your heart"—I pointed to her heart; she looked down at her chest—"and all you'll have left is a hateful heart."

She gave me a serious look and shook her head. "*I'm* not gonna get hungry. *I'm* just gonna hate Alvina."

So much for my lesson.

"Tell you what," I said. "Before you start hating Alvina, let's give her another chance."

"What for?"

"Because I think she's got a problem."

"What kind of problem?"

"I think she's angry."

Her eyes rode up to mine. "What's she angry at? The boy?"

"I don't know," I said. "Maybe the boy. Maybe something else. Maybe she's just having growing pains."

"Growing pains? What's that?"

"It's when a little kid is becoming a big kid. Sometimes it hurts."

"Will I have growing pains?"

"Maybe just a teeny one."

"Am I gonna beat up a boy?"

I lifted her down to the sidewalk. We headed for home. "I certainly hope not," I said.

May 21

I invited myself and Dootsie to dinner at Betty Lou's today. We got there mid-afternoon so we could help her make her famous cheese-and-garlic smashed potatoes—more specifically, so Dootsie could smash the potatoes.

As soon as Betty Lou and I settled into peeling the spuds, Betty Lou said, "So. How was the Dogwood Festival? I want to hear all about it."

Dootsie piped, "Alvina beat up a boy!"

Betty Lou turned to me. I nodded. "Sad but true."

"Did she hurt him?" said Betty Lou.

"He was bleeding," said Dootsie. "I cried."

"It was over in a minute," I said. "People pulled them apart."

"Alvina's a pip," said Dootsie.

Betty Lou gave a sad smile and wagged her head. "That she is."

Dootsie said, "I wanna be a pip."

Betty Lou swallowed her in a hug and laughed aloud. "You *are* a pip, my little pip-squeak. Now tell me about the festival. How about the Dogwood Queen? Was she beautiful?"

"I got lots of candy!" said Dootsie.

"She was beautiful," I said.

"I was a piggy and a bully!"

Betty Lou nodded knowingly. "The Queen always is beautiful. She's always a senior girl from the high school, you know. On Friday she's just another student in the hallways. And on Saturday"—her fists bloomed into fingers—"*poof!*—she's up there on the backseat of a shiny bright convertible, smiling down on her people, waving. A Queen. Perfect."

She was looking out the kitchen window. She was seeing festivals past, Queens of other Mays.

"I gave it all away!" shouted Dootsie.

Betty Lou smiled at the window. "I was in the Queen's Court, in case you didn't know."

I was shocked. "Betty Lou! You were?"

"Oh yes. I wasn't beautiful enough to be Queen, of course. But I was a bit of a looker in my own right." She gave me a sly grin. "Believe it or not."

"Oh, I *do* believe," I told her quickly, before my eyes, seeing the lady in red slipper socks and purple bathrobe and gray hair across the table, had a chance to contradict me.

"We were called Blossoms then. The Queen and her six

Blossoms." She stuck out her tongue and made a gagging sound. "You believe it? Sounds so quaint now, doesn't it? Well, it *is* a problem, isn't it? What were they supposed to call us—the Queen and her six Losers? So silly. But then— I'll tell you, Stargirl—then I took my role as a Blossom quite seriously. Quite seriously." She broke out laughing. "Ha! To the point of unseemliness, my mother would say. She had to practically rip my gown off my body when I went to bed that night."

She sat herself on the edge of the table. She looked about—and suddenly she was no longer in the kitchen, she was in the parade, waving, smiling, blowing kisses. Dootsie and I applauded. Betty Lou returned to the present, looked at us. "You know, you haven't lived until you've basked in the adoration of the people."

As Betty Lou busied herself at the oven, my thoughts went back to the Mica High prom about this time last year. Any regrets, Leo? Do you wish you had gone with me? I'm sure you've heard all about it by now. That crazy Stargirl showing up in a chauffeur-driven bicycle. Dancing with herself, then all the guys. And the bunny hop. Leading them off the lantern-lit tennis courts into the dark. Here's the truth, Leo. Until the bunny hop, I was doing fine. I was enjoying myself and my schoolmates, putting you and your rejection of me aside. But out there in the dark, the farther we got from the music and the light, the more I thought of you, and it occurred to me that maybe I could work a little enchantment of my own. As we moved deeper and deeper into the dark I wished—I *willed*—that something magical would happen, that the hands I felt on my waist, if I danced through the darkness just right and just long enough, would become your hands.

But of course they didn't. When we came back to the light and I looked, it was Alan Ferko behind me, not you.

By now Dootsie had made herself disappear. She does that if she thinks she's not getting enough attention. She stood in the corner, eyes squeezed shut, noiseless, still as a floor lamp—Cinnamon visible as usual on her shoulder.

"Where's Dootsie?" Betty Lou said with a wink.

I looked around. I looked straight into the corner. I shrugged. "Don't know. She must have disappeared again. Looks like she took Cinnamon with her this time."

Betty Lou called, "Dootsie? Are you here?"

Silence from the corner.

"How does she *do* it?" said Betty Lou, wonderment in her voice.

"It's a gift," I said.

"Do you think we'll ever see her again?" Betty Lou said worriedly.

"When she's ready," I said.

Betty Lou nodded, relieved. "Good. So then, tell me about the rest of the Dogwood Festival."

I told her about it all, painted her a picture as best I could. In the meantime, the smells of roasting turkey breast and tofurkey (yes, tofu turkey—I'm still a vegetarian) filled the house. I thought I saw a nose appear in the corner just long enough to sniff.

When I finished, Betty Lou again gazed out the window. "Do you think I'll ever see another Dogwood Festival?" She turned to me. Her eyes were gleaming. "Do you, Girl of the Stars?"

I wanted to cry. Across the kitchen table we squeezed each other's hands. "You will," I told her, not sure I believed myself.

Betty Lou checked the big pot on the stove. "Uh-oh. The potatoes are ready to be smashed and Dootsie the Super Potato Smasher is nowhere to be seen."

"I'm here! I'm here!" Dootsie came bursting into visibility, Cinnamon hanging on to her shoulder for dear life. "I'll smash 'em!" She started pulling off her shoes.

She had to be talked out of doing it with her feet. She had seen a picture of winemakers stomping grapes. Then she had to be talked out of letting Cinnamon stomp.

At last the potatoes got smashed, and the dinner was eaten. I took Dootsie home. The last thing she said when I hugged her good night was, "I wanna do a festible!"

May 26

So we had the Dootsie Festival today.

Like the Dogwood Festival, it began with a parade. Dootsie appointed Cinnamon Grand Marshal and herself "Boss Queen." She was wrapped in dish towels. She seemed to think this was glamorous. She wore her mother's high heels and a white plastic comb in her hair that she called a crown. I pulled her along in a little wooden wagon. She smiled and waved to the crowd (about ten parents) along Ringgold Street. The Grand Marshal sat on her shoulder.

She was trailed by three attendants, walking—no wagons for them. Two were little girls from the neighborhood. The third was a black Lab named Roscoe. I told Dootsie it was a boy dog, but she didn't care. Roscoe wore a pink crinoline ballet skirt.

The rest of the parade consisted of a boy with a turtle, a little kid on a tricycle, a marching band (two ten-year-olds playing a harmonica and a kazoo but mostly goofing off), a three-foot-high Darth Vader, a grandmother holding the hand of a wide-eyed toddler, and a teenager doing wheelies on his skateboard.

After one block, the Boss Queen called, "Parade's over!" and we all returned to her house to have the festival.

We had attractions galore: bake sale, fortune-teller, penny pitch, stroller coaster. And of course a lemonade stand. I even gave a ukulele concert.

The Grand Marshal tried to get some shut-eye in a bicycle basket, but tiny hands petting kept him awake.

I'm sure everything was being watched by Betty Lou, though I couldn't see her.

The festival was hopping when I saw him on the sidewalk out front. The face from the Dumpster. Betty Lou's porch. The caramel apple stand.

He was talking to the lemonade vendor, the Boss Queen herself. They were chatting away. She poured him a cup of lemonade and he dropped a nickel into the cash register (her Babar cereal bowl). I kept my eyes on his hands, expecting one of them at any moment to slip into the bowl and take something out. I wondered if he was chatting her up to distract her. I wondered if the moment she turned her back he would snatch the bowl as he did the donuts and the caramel apple. But the only thing happening was talk. He was gesturing with his hands, telling her a story. She was laughing and saying things back to him. In fact, they were having such a great old time that suddenly I felt a twinge of jealousy that Dootsie—my little Dootsie—was so instantly smitten with this new boy person.

My impulse was to stride right over there and reclaim my territory, let her show him who her best pal was. But I hesitated. I had seen him so clearly three times—three times stealing (well, two—or can you steal from a Dumpster?)—that I felt I must be as memorable to him as he was to me. But when he looked up from the lemonade table and his eyes drifted in my direction, he didn't seem to recognize me. He had black hair that flopped down to his eyes and over his ears. His skin looked as if it had been toasted in the Arizona desert. Even at a distance I could see his eyes were blue.

He pulled a pair of sunglasses—shoplifted, no doubt—from his pocket and put them on. I saw Dootsie's hands shoot out and heard her exclaim: "Me! Me!" He put them on her. *She let him*, I thought. *She wouldn't let me put my earrings on her.* She stood up. She strutted down the sidewalk. She turned and looked straight into the sun. "Dootsie!" I called, but he was already there, turning her face aside, taking the glasses, scolding her for looking into the sun. I was outraged. *Hey*, I wanted to call out, *I'll do the scolding around here.*

He held his hand out. They shook. He was saying goodbye. *Please don't hug her*, I thought. His hand went to the top of her head and mussed her hair. She laughed. He walked up the street.

I followed him.

Even now I'm not sure why. I stayed a block or two behind, on the other side of the street.

It was a long walk, back through downtown, past Margie's Donuts and Pizza Dee-Lite and the Colonial Theatre and the Morning Lenape Building and the Blue Comet diner and the Columbia Hotel and over the canal bridge. When he came to Produce Junction he veered into the parking lot. Boxes of fruit and vegetables were on display outside the door. He snatched two lemons as he breezed by and headed on down Canal Street. He stuck one lemon in his pocket. He broke the other one and started sucking on a half. Just watching him, my spit dried up. I walked faster. He was breezing along in his shades, more swaggering than walking, sucking on his lemon, spitting seeds into the street like he owned the world. I felt my bile rising. I was still twenty feet behind when he turned toward a small gray cinder-blocky building on the canal. The side facing the canal was open like a garage. Above the opening a hand-painted sign said IKE'S BIKE & MOWER REPAIR. Ike was bending in the dirt outside, pulling the cord on a mower and cursing every time it didn't start. The boy went around the side and up two steps to a back door.

I called, "Hey!"

He looked up, his hand on the doorknob. He didn't speak, just waited. He didn't remove his sunglasses. The longer he stood there, the more uncomfortable I became that he could see my eyes but I couldn't see his.

I came closer. "Why did you take those lemons?" I said. "Why do you steal things?"

No answer. No expression. I felt if I could tear off his shades I would find two cold blue stones. He tossed the half lemon away and shoved the whole other half into his mouth. He worked it around and his lips puckered, and suddenly he spat a seed at me. It bounced off my chest. He stood there chewing with his mouth open. I thought I saw a tiny sneer on his lip just before he opened the door and went in.

May 28

I finally have a name for the boy, the lemon thief. Perry. He doesn't look like a Perry to me, but that's what he told Dootsie his name is. He also told her he sleeps on the roof on hot nights. And he fishes in the canal. And sometimes he swims in it even though no one is supposed to.

Dootsie told me all this as we were having lunch at the Blue Comet. The treat was on her—some of it, anyway. With her profits from the festival—$11.27—she insisted on taking me to lunch.

"So," I said, "what else did he say?"

She licked ketchup from a French fry. "I don't remember. Stuff."

"I saw you laughing."

"Yeah. He was funny."

"And nice?"

"Uh-huh."

When she finished licking the French fry clean, she started in on another.

"If all you want is the ketchup," I said, "why did you order French fries?"

She sighed, trying to be patient. "Because you can't just *drink* ketchup, you goof."

We hung around downtown for a while, then we went to Margie's for afternoon dessert. Dootsie got plain-with-sprinkles, I got chocolate-glazed. As we sat down Alvina came barging through the door. She waved at me. "Hey, wacko. Do anything wacky today?"

Dootsie whispered, "Is she gonna beat you up?"

I whispered back, "I don't think so."

"Is she gonna beat *me* up?"

"She's not going to beat anybody up. Relax. Eat your donut."

Alvina took her books into the back and came out with her broom. "You're not gonna sit here the whole day nursing that one donut, are ya?" she said.

"Maybe I am," I said. "You got a problem??" I might have even snarled.

I felt Dootsie rising beside me. "Yeah. You got a *probum?*" She *was* snarling. Red and blue sprinkles fell from the half-eaten donut that she wagged in Alvina's face.

Alvina stared stone-faced—and quick as a lemon thief, she tore the half donut from Dootsie's hand and popped it into her mouth.

Dootsie howled. "Margie! She stole my donut!"

Margie called from the counter, "Good grief. You're three immature babies over there." She plucked another plain-with-sprinkles from the rack and tossed it our way. "Here. Now shut up, all of you, or I'll kick you out."

I caught the donut and gave it to Dootsie, who stuck her sprinkle-crusted tongue out at Alvina, who went off sweeping.

When Alvina finished her sweeping, she came and sat at our table.

"I don't like you," said Dootsie.

"Dootsie," I said, "be nice."

But Dootsie was rolling. "When I get big enough, I'm gonna beat *you* up."

Alvina looked at her across the table. Her face was as stony as ever. I have known her for months now and have never seen her smile. And yet something was there, under the surface, behind her eyes, on the edge of her lips, something softer, something little. Her hand slowly formed a fist and slowly came across the table until it stopped a quarter inch in front of Dootsie's nose. Dootsie's eyes crossed as they followed it in. Tucked into the fist was the elegant pink nail on the little finger.

Dootsie jerked back—but only to protect her new donut. She held it behind her chair. She was not the least bit afraid of Alvina. Their eyes were locked into each other's, but they showed neither fear nor hatred. Their stares were more probing than clashing. Dootsie brought her face forward until it was again in front of the fist. She opened her mouth as wide as she could and, still staring up into Alvina's eyes, closed her teeth slowly, gently, on Alvina's knuckles. Alvina did not pull away. Dootsie did not bite down hard. Something was happening that I didn't understand, and somehow that made it all the more special. I looked at Margie. She was staring, openmouthed, the coffee urn in her hand poised above a cup. When I turned back, Dootsie was releasing her bite and Alvina laid her hand flat upon the table.

Margie's voice broke the spell: "Alvina. Back to work."

Alvina grabbed her broom and headed for the kitchen in back.

May 31

When I tried to do my mind wash today, a smidgen of me would not evaporate away. It was those stone blue eyes behind the sunglasses and the lemon seed bouncing off my shirt. For today at least, I guess I flunked Elements of Nothingness.

June 4

FIELD TRIP:
MAIDEN'S LEAP
She stood here, the Lenape girl.
She was only thirteen or fourteen,
the legend says.
Here on this high bluff overlooking the ramshackle remains
of the old steel mill
famous in the Revolution for making the best
cannon for George Washington's army.
Of course it wasn't a steel plant then,
just forest,
maybe rocks.
She stood here and then she jumped . . .
well, perhaps *leaped*, since this is a
poem and *leaped* feels more poetic
than *jumped*.

In any case, down she went to her death,
thirteen- or fourteen-year-old Lenape girl,
because her father would not allow her to marry
the boy she loved.

Standing here, I wonder things.
I wonder if she started way back there and
came running and practically flew
off the edge.
Or did she come slowly, like a trickle of water
across a tabletop that seems to pause
at the edge, gathering itself
before spilling?
If she did stand here and wait—why?
What was she waiting for?
Was she giving time one last chance
to save her? Happiness one last chance
to happen?
Ha! Easier to rearrange the stars than
a father's mind.
Did she look down?
Did she look out?
What did she see?
Did she see his face? The boy's?
Did she see him wave to her, call to her
from far away? Did she see the two
of them running, laughing across meadows
of chicory and Queen Anne's lace, flowers they knew

by other names?
And his name—did she say it?
Did she shout it from the blufftop to
all the earth below?
Or whisper it, for his ears only
to hear?
One thing for sure—it comes clearly now:
she was not looking down.
This I know.

June 5

Homeschool is out!

At high noon I celebrated by joining you for smoothies at the mall. Strawberry-banana, of course. Your favorite. We sat together at the last table and talked and sipped. I told you the latest with Dootsie. You brought me up-to-date on your friend Kevin and my friend Dori Dilson and our friend Archie. You told me you're looking forward to summer vacation. You told me you applied to colleges in Pennsylvania, since now you know this is where I am. You said you think of me every day. You said you sometimes go out to the enchanted place in the desert and take off your shoes and sit there like we did that first time. Only you don't meditate. You're not at all interested in erasing your self or me. Oh no. Just the opposite. You close your eyes and you remember. You focus and you concentrate and you remember harder than you've ever remembered in your life, and pretty soon you're sure you can feel me there, sitting cross-legged across from you, smiling at you, Cinnamon in the space between us. You experience me. You relive us. You're so happy. And then so sad when you open your eyes and realize I'm not really there. That's when you miss me the most. Desperately.

Tell me I didn't imagine it, Leo. Tell me that even though our bodies were in separate states, our star selves shared an enchanted place. Tell me that right around noon today (eastern time) you had the strangest sensation: a tiny chill on your shoulder . . . a flutter in the heart . . . a shadow of strawberry-banana crossing your tongue. . . .

Tell me you whispered my name.

June 12

Last night's dream . . .

Milk run. Bottles rattle in the racks. Headlights swing through the darkness. *There* . . . someone in a Dumpster . . . head down, rummaging . . . looks up, eyes gleaming like a surprised fox's . . . but it's not that boy Perry . . . it's you.

June 15

I keep thinking about Charlie at the cemetery. Sitting there day after day. Talking to Grace. Remembering. Dozing off. I think he must hate the absolute certainty: knowing that every time he awakes from a doze, she'll be there. Every time he arrives in the morning with the aluminum chair, she'll be there. She'll never again be in the basement looking for the canned peaches. Never again out in the backyard chatting with Mrs. So-and-So, the neighbor. She'll never be anywhere but *there*.

Does it make you wonder, Leo? Someday in the far future, when the Milky Way has turned another cosmic click, will someone carry a chair to your grave site and keep you company forever? Can you imagine someone loving you that much? Can I?

And I'm thinking maybe I did the donut thing all wrong. How was he supposed to know what was in the bag? Or that the donuts were for him? He probably thought it was just litter and in the name of Grace booted it away.

So this time I'll do it differently. I got a small white wicker basket. I put in three donuts. I covered the donuts with plastic wrap so he could see what was there. I'll sneak out early tomorrow morning, à la Dootsie, while it's still dark, and leave the basket by the tombstone.

June 16

He took it!

I rode to the cemetery this afternoon. I was nervous. I pedaled around behind him. I kept my distance. At first I didn't see it. Then I changed my angle—and there it was, the white basket, sitting in the grass beside his foot. He was nodding off, his chin in his chest. I was so happy I gave a little "Yippee!" as I pedaled away.

June 18

Here's the new ad I put in the *Morning Lenape* today. I don't know if he reads the paper. I decided it would be safer not to use names:

Every day he visits her,
talks with her,
sleeps with her.

June 21

Summer Solstice.

When you woke up this morning, dear Leo, the sun was directly above the Tropic of Cancer. You will never find it any farther north. This is the longest day of the year. From now until the Winter Solstice on December 21, each day will be a few minutes shorter than the one before. Today is the official beginning of summer.

In other words, it's a holiday. Not a people holiday—a natural holiday. And who wants to celebrate a holiday alone? And since you're not here, I thought: OK—*Dootsie*.

When I told her about it last week, the first thing she said was, "Let's get dressed up!" Amazing how this little kid is always one step ahead of me. We went to my mother's workroom. My mother dove into the remnant pile of her recent costume-making jobs, stitched together some pieces, and voilà: Dootsie looking like she flew through a rainbow. As for me, I got out the buttercup dress I wore to the Ocotillo Ball. (You remember, don't you? The ball you didn't ask me to.)

I decided to do it, naturally enough, on Enchanted Hill. Dootsie stayed over at my house last night. My mother had told her parents what I had in mind. They had no problem with Dootsie sleeping over, but they were a little shaky on her going outside while it was still dark, even for such a short distance, even with me. So my mother volunteered my father.

"He'll drive them in the milk truck," she told them.

"Won't he be late for work?" they said.

"It happens now and then," she said. "The customers understand. Acts of God and nature. Snow. Ice. Crazy daughter."

"Okay," they said.

Dootsie was limp as a rag doll when I dressed her at 4:30 a.m. As usual, my mother came down to the porch, walkie-talkie in the pocket of her bathrobe. Turning on the porch light, I noticed that the porch light of our next-door neighbors, the Cantellos, was also on.

We loaded Dootsie and her little wooden wagon—the one that had carried Boss Queen in the parade—into the truck and rattled off to Enchanted Hill. A whole minute later my father parked the truck at the weedy edge of the field, near the white stucco bungalow, and carried the wagon and bath mat while I toted the little sleeper. The earth was lumpy as always, but softer now than during the winter. I didn't use my flashlight. The quarter moon, and my father, were enough.

My father put down the wagon and stood beside me facing the horizon. It was still too dark to tell where earth stopped and sky began. He reached for my hand. He turned to us. He touched Dootsie's face. He brought us into his arms and held us, Dootsie breathing so deeply between us it seemed she herself was generating the night. I felt his lips through my hair. He gave me a final squeeze on the arm and walked away toward the two red dots that marked the truck in the distance.

I sat down in the dark and cradled Dootsie like a baby, swinging her gently, humming a lullaby accompanied by the swish of our dresses rubbing together. When night began to fade in the east, I woke her. "Come on. Sunny Sun is coming. We have to be ready." I stood her on her feet and forced her to walk around the field until she was fully awake.

"Where is it?" she said.

"It's coming," I told her. The sky in the east was gray now, the little stucco bungalow was coming into view. I pointed. "See? Keep watching." I straddled the wagon behind her. "See?" I whispered in her ear. "It gets lighter and lighter. The colors change . . . see . . . see . . ."

I said no more. We watched the sky turn from pearly

gray to powder blue . . . and *there* . . . out beyond, 90 million miles beyond, a brightening, a mist of lighter light, a puff . . . *there . . . now!* . . . and suddenly I was up and running, as I realized I was on the wrong end of the sled, I was missing something maybe even grander than the sunrise itself. I ran straight for the sun. I didn't worry about Dootsie, because I knew she never even noticed that I had left the wagon. Then I turned and looked back and saw . . . and that's as far as words will take me. So I'll fall back to this: I saw a little girl in a wooden wagon, her dress spilling colors over its sides, staring at the rising sun as if it were the very dawn of creation. As I walked toward her I had no urge to turn around and see the sunrise myself, for I was already looking at everything I needed to see. She never moved as I came closer and closer, until I could see the growing glint of the rising sun doubled in her eyes.

I resumed my seat on the wagon behind her. Halfway born, the sun lost its edge and its orange and flooded the east with blinding yellow. I picked her up and propped her on my shoulders, the proper place to greet the sunrise. I looked to the edge of the field—the milk truck was gone. I walked her around. Neither of us wanted to leave. Only the sun inching up from the horizon gave hint that time was passing. As we meandered, she said my name three times:

"Stargirl?"

"Yes?"

"That was better than TV."

"It was."

"Stargirl?"

"Yes?"

"Does the sun do that every day?"

"Yes."

"Stargirl?"

"Yes?"

"Every day is sun day."

All dressed up for Summer Solstice—it seemed a waste to just walk straight home. So I walkie-talkied my mother and told her we were taking the long way. At first the streets were empty, except for the drivers delivering copies of the *Morning Lenape*. The folded papers seemed to leap on their own from the car windows. By the time the sun sat atop the chimneys, school buses were rumbling past and women in robes and slippers were slinking forth to pick up their papers. We waved to everyone we saw. I wondered what they thought: a big girl pulling a little girl in a wagon, both dolled up as if going to a prom or wedding. I like to think we gave them a happy start to the longest day.

June 28

It was more like a mind rinse than a mind wash at Enchanted Hill this morning. I couldn't stop remembering, even refeeling, the magic of last week, of Dootsie's eyes. I sense the wonder still haunting the hill, hungry for more eyes.

June 29

I got a letter from Archie today. I miss him a lot. Some of my happiest memories are of sitting with Archie on his back porch, rocking in the chair, gazing at the purple Maricopas through his pipe smoke (don't you love that cherry smell?), talking his ears off about you. He liked you—I didn't allow him not to—but even then I could tell he had his doubts about my choice of boyfriend. You remember how crushed I was when nobody showed up to greet me after I won the oratorical contest—well, that was nothing to how bad I felt when I saw his reaction to my trading in Stargirl for conventional Susan. The look in his eyes when I told him— that was maybe the low point in my life. I hope I never hurt anyone like that again. Even so, he wanted to blame you. He believed you pressured me to betray myself. I tried to tell him no, it was my choice. I was a big girl and I knew what I was doing; it was no crime to be popular. He pretended to understand and accept, because he loved me that much, but he would never call me Susan, and I never saw him happier than the day I told him I had decided to become Stargirl again.

As for you, I think he feels conflicted. He wants to like you. He does like you. You get automatic points for being the boy in my heart. And he knows that the better part of you didn't give up without a fight. On the other hand, I think he still secretly blames you for my self-betrayal. He doesn't think you're—in his word—"ready" for me. He says in his letter he deliberately threw you off the trail by telling you we moved to Minnesota, not Pennsylvania. I had to laugh at that.

He tells me you still attend meetings of the Loyal Order of the Stone Bone. He tells me that he showed you my "office" in his toolshed. (I was hoping he would.) He says you were properly impressed. He says you appeared to be truly touched. He says there may be hope for you after all.

July 4

The Caraways and the Pringles spent the Fourth together. The two families are friends now, thanks to their daughters. We went to the parade. I love the marching bands best. Dootsie and I held our ears and screamed when the sirening fire trucks went by. It was very hot. There was no shade. Mr. Pringle had a plastic spritzer bottle. He kept spraying his face. Dootsie didn't even notice the heat, but she kept snatching the bottle anyway until she used up all the water before the parade was half over. Mr. Pringle was not happy.

We barbecued chicken and hot dogs and veggie burgers on the Pringles' patio and did our eating in the air-conditioned den. Don't ask me how he did it, but in my honor Mr. Pringle even barbecued some smashed potatoes.

At night we watched the fireworks at the American Legion baseball field. Dootsie and I sat toboggan-style on a blanket as we watched the colors burst and spill across the sky. Thousands of upturned faces flashed in the night, people on blankets and lawn chairs, gasping together at the bursting, pulpy pearls, utterly silent between the cannon shots of the high boomers. It seemed the whole town was there—except for Betty Lou. I wondered if she could see from a window. I wondered about the lost man in the moss-green pullover cap. And Grace's Charlie. And Alvina. And Perry. Were they all looking up, enthralled with the rest of us?

July 5

When I went to Enchanted Hill this morning, I carried more than the usual flashlight, walkie-talkie, and bath mat. I also took:

50 ft of rope

a croquet stake

a heavy hammer

a spatula

Here's what I did: I pounded the stake into the middle of the field. I tied one end of the rope around the stake and walked the other end toward the eastern horizon and waited for the sun. As soon as it appeared, I used the rope to make a straight line between stake and sun. Then, at the end of the rope, I planted the spatula in the ground.

Have you figured it out yet? I'm making a calendar. Sort of like Stonehenge. It's the way our ancestors kept track of themselves in time. Every Thursday I'll plant another spatula. (I bought a bunch of them at the dollar store. They look like little white rubbery paddles.) Twenty-four Thursdays from now, on December 20, I'll plant the last one. By then the spatulas will form an arc, a quarter circle. The arc will trace the path of the rising sun as it appears above the horizon a little later each week. December 21 is the day I'm aiming for: Winter Solstice. It's the shortest day of the year, the day the sun turns from its northward path and begins to move south. It's the official beginning of winter, but in a sense it's also the true beginning of summer, because from December 21 on, each day will be a little longer than the one before.

But ancient people were never sure that was going to happen from year to year. They were afraid the light might keep getting less and less and finally disappear. That's why they had Solstice celebrations, to persuade the sun to turn around and come back.

I'm going to have a Winter Solstice celebration. I'm going to invite people. Maybe the suspense is gone, but the wonder in Dootsie's eyes—that's what I want to share.

July 6

Three days in a row over 90—it's officially a heat wave. And it's worse than Arizona heat. No wonder you moved from Pennsylvania. Pennsylvania heat is not only hot, it's soggy. It's like walking around in hot oatmeal. It's like sitting on a steaming teakettle. It's . . . oh, never mind, I can see I'm not getting any sympathy from you.

So I was cooling off in the library today, sitting at the end of a table, reading poems by Mary Oliver, when I caught a tiny flying movement out of the corner of my eye. And a tiny sound: *plit.* From where I sat I could look up the aisle to where the book stacks ended. It seemed to have come from between two of the stacks. And there it was again, about fifteen feet away, flying out from between the stacks—it looked like a seed—*plit* against the library window. I didn't need three guesses. *That boy,* I thought. *Perry.*

When the third *plit* came a minute later, I'd had enough. I slammed my book down and stomped up the aisle. There he was, sitting cross-legged on the floor between the stacks, blocking the way, reading a book, sucking on a lemon. I stood there, glaring down at him. At first I thought he was simply ignoring me. As the seconds went by, I became less sure. He seemed totally swallowed up in the book. A sucked-out rind of a half lemon lay on the floor. The other half was moving around in his mouth.

Frankly, I was surprised he wasn't reading a comic. It was a real book. Of course, it wasn't much of a book. It was thin. I couldn't see the title. This was frustrating to me, because whenever I see somebody reading a book I *have* to see the title. Sometimes when this happens on a train or in a waiting room, I can get downright rude as I try to get into position to see the cover. But first things first. "I know you know I'm standing here," I said.

His head jerked up, his blue eyes wide—a perfect imitation of a surprised person. "You win the Oscar," I said.

"Huh?" he said, still putting on the surprised act.

"Never mind. You're spitting seeds again. It's one thing outside. This—"

He spat another one: *pthoo*.

"—is a *library*." I kicked his foot.

He kicked me back. I was shocked. It hurt. I snatched the book from his hands. It was called *Ondine*. A play by a French writer.

He snatched it back. I tried to give him my most wicked stare, which made me feel kind of silly since I haven't had much practice at that kind of thing. And my stare was wasted anyway, since his nose was back into the book and he resumed his portrayal of the Reader Who Doesn't Know There's a Person Standing in Front of Him.

It occurred to me that there wasn't a thing left for me to do but walk away. So I did. And came right back and pointed at him and said, "And stay away from Dootsie."

He never looked up.

July 7

I have to say, *Ondine* is just about the last thing I would expect that kid to be reading. It's a play about a girl who is not just a girl, she's something like a mermaid. We might call her magical or fantastic, but I think more than anything else she is simply human. She sees with the eyes of a child. She is happy and forever singing. She lives with an old couple in the forest by a lake, and when a knight named Hans comes by, she thinks he is the most beautiful creature she has ever seen. She wants nothing more than to be his wife and to live happily ever after. But it's not as simple as that. She has been fished up into a world that does not understand its Ondines. In the end the people reject her and banish her to the waters from which she came. Her beloved Hans dies on the shore. Mercifully, her memory of him is erased, and when she later sees him from the water she is struck anew by his beauty and she cries out: "How I should have loved him!"

Why was he reading this? Why was he reading at all? How could he be reading a book that, now that I've read it too, turns out to be my favorite of all time?

July 9

I woke up to a frantic phone call from Dootsie: "Hurry! There's a red slipper in Betty Lou's window!"

Ten minutes later we were in her living room. First thing I did was take the red slipper sock from the front window.

"Sorry," she said, slumped on the sofa. "I didn't mean to bother you. Sometimes it just gets to me."

"Hey," I said, "that's what good friends are for—bad days."

Betty Lou was forbidden to work, but she was allowed to give directions, and that's how Dootsie and I, master pastry

chefs, managed to bake a batch of chocolate chip cookies.
We fed her, combed her hair, massaged her feet, read to her,
sang to her, danced for her, and by dinnertime she was dancing along with us.

July 11

Did I tell you?—I'm a working girl. I call myself the Garden
Groomer. I put a sign in Margie's window and an ad in the
Lenape classifieds. Mr. Pringle made me some business cards
on his computer. My logo is a worm with a baseball cap and
a big smile. I'm not a flower expert, so I don't do anything
fancy. Just simple stuff—weed, water, deadhead. And I'm
cheap. That's probably the main reason I get jobs. That and
my ultra-cool wheelbarrow. I bought it at the hardware
store. I painted my worm on one side and a sunflower on the
other.

Today I was at the house of a family named Klecko. Mrs.
Klecko had called me last week. The house is beautiful, gray
stone with a wraparound porch and yellow awnings, on a
street shaded by sycamores.

I went right to the back, which is part brick patio, part
grass, and the most beautiful garden I've worked on so far.
The flowers alone would have been enough, but there was
more—elegant grasses taller than me, little stone sculptures
(a child reading, a garden angel), a white birch and a pair of
holly trees, a flagstone path winding through it all. As I've
told you before, enchanted places cannot be created, they

can only be discovered—but the Kleckos' garden comes pretty close.

The first thing I did was pick up the plastic toys and toss them onto the grass. Obviously, a little kid lived here—a boy, judging from the army tank and water pistol. Then I started in on the deadheading. (Sounds gruesome, but all it means is snipping off dead flowers, so the plant can direct all of its energy to the living.) I was pulling off some coneflowers when I heard an agonized scream coming from the house. Then a second scream. Then a voice: "I'll kill you!" And another voice: "I'll tell Mommy!"

I was debating whether to go into the house and thinking that first voice sounded familiar when a brown-haired little boy in nothing but Batman underpants shot out the back door screaming and made a beeline for me. He was followed a second later by none other than . . . Alvina!

The boy crashed into me and swung around behind me, hugging me, his ear buried in my rear end, his arms wrapped around my hips. Alvina came up short when she recognized me.

"What are you doing here?" she snarled.

"I'm grooming the garden," I said. "Do you live here?" I realized I had never known her last name.

"No," she sneered. "I'm Goldilocks. I just snuck into Baby Bear's bed."

She reached for the boy. I saw that her hand was bleeding. He dug his fingers into my waist. She kicked him. He howled—and kicked her back. She howled.

"Stop!" I shrieked, surprising myself. This was a quiet neighborhood.

I peeled the boy off and made him face me. I growled at Alvina, "Back off." She glared hatefully at me but backed off. "Is this your brother?"

"*It's* the pimple on my butt," she said.

"She's the pimple on *my* butt!" the boy retorted.

"Enough!" I said. "What's your name?"

He said it as if spitting at her: "Thomas!"

To Alvina: "Where's your mother?"

"At the dentist."

"So you're supposed to be watching him?"

"Watching *it*," she sneered.

Alvina's breath came in hissy snorts. Her teeth were bared like a snarling dog's. This was vintage Alvina. What surprised me was the little brother. Sure, he was cowering, but only in a pound-for-pound-mismatch sort of way. He was no more afraid of her than Dootsie had been in Margie's. I thought: *Alvina, when he gets bigger, you're in trouble.*

"Your brother is a *he*," I said, "not an *it*."

"*It's* gonna be dead as soon as you get outta here," she said.

"Then I'm not going till your mother gets back."

Thomas crowed, "Yeah!" He took a step forward and flicked out a bare leg at her. She came for him. I jabbed my finger in her face. I tried to look stern. "Stay!"

He laughed. "Yeah! Stay, doggie!"

Before I knew what was happening, he turned around,

bent over, pulled down his little black and yellow Batmans and mooned his sister. This was clearly nothing new to Alvina. She showed neither shock nor disgust. She simply reared back and spat on the moon. He screamed bloody murder and pulled up his Batmans and rubbed his hiney. Alvina seemed to sense the advantage. Again she came forward. I put out my hand like a crossing guard. "Alvina—not another step."

She stopped, gave me a sneery grin. "Yeah? What're you gonna do? *Hit* me?"

What *was* I going to do? I had no idea. Tickle her? We locked eyes for the longest time. Finally she blinked. Her face changed. She jabbed her hand at me. "Look what he did!"

Her little finger was bleeding, the one with the elegant nail, only now it was an un-elegant stub.

"What happened?" I said.

"He chopped it," she said, whining now, telling me the whole gruesome story. He had gotten hold of his father's nail clippers. As soon as their mother left, he started clipping himself: fingernails, toenails, eyebrows, eyelashes. Since he was doing this at the breakfast table, Alvina took her cereal down to the basement den. Which is where she was sometime later, nestled in the arms of her father's super-duper reclining easy chair, watching Comedy Central, except not really watching it, because that easy chair for some reason has the strangest effect on her—whenever she climbs into it she wants to doze off. And that's what she was doing, not really sleeping but just nodding off in the chair, half hearing the TV sounds, when suddenly she heard a snippy little noise and felt a little tug on her little finger and she opened her eyes and there was Thomas with a mile-wide grin on his face, holding up a full half inch of pink, glittery fingernail that he had just clipped off. Which was bad enough, but that wasn't all. So shocked was she at the sight of her mutilated fingernail that her hand shot out and knocked her father's bowling trophy from the side table onto the floor, where it broke in half. Which was bad *enough*, except that her hand hit the sharp edge of the trophy base and came away with a nasty, bleeding cut. Which is when the screaming started.

I got most of the story as I dragged her into the house, asking her where's the bathroom, where's the medicine cabinet, Batman pattering after us—"Is she gonna bleed to death?"—putting her hand under the running water, rubbing on Neosporin. I sat on the edge of the bathtub. The cut was so long I had to use overlapping Band-Aids. "Show this to your mom," I told her. "She might want you to get a tetanus shot."

She didn't answer. I hadn't been looking at her. Now I did. Her lip was quivering. A tear—a real crying-type tear—was rolling down her cheek. She was staring at her lopped-off fingernail. I stood and hugged her. I thought she might resist, but she didn't. Batman gaped at us. "You loved your fingernail, didn't you?" I said softly. Her head nodded against me. I looked at Thomas. "Batman," I said, "go get some clothes on." He ran off.

As we walked back down the hallway, we passed something I had been too preoccupied to notice before: a double-life-size cardboard cutout of the snarling face of a pit bull. It was tacked to a door. "Your room?" I said.

"Yeah," she said.

Nosy me: "Going to invite me in?"

She pushed the door open. I went in. I had to step around a scattered deck of cards, a pile of poker chips, and a hockey stick on the floor. In a corner: a one-legged teddy bear, its head lost in a football helmet. Tacked to the wall was the front page from a gag newspaper with the headline:

ALVINA KLECKO CROWNED
NEW HEAVYWEIGHT CHAMP

Hanging from a bedpost: a pair of black nunchucks. No frills. No pink. But . . . on a shelf above the head of the bed: a lineup of dolls. They seemed to go from the youngest on one end to the oldest on the other, from baby to glamorous model. Several were Barbies. I counted them—there were eleven. One for each birthday, I guessed.

I kept looking at the dolls, trying to make them fit with the girl I thought I knew. I would have expected them to be G.I. Joes and Hulks and Terminators.

I looked at her. *"Barbies?"* I said.

"You got a problem?" she said, ending that discussion.

She pulled the clipped-off half inch of pink fingernail from her pocket. She fitted it to the end of the remaining stub. "Can it be fixed?" Her voice was peepy.

"We'll see," I said. "We'll do something about it."

She looked at it some more. Her expression hardened. She threw the clipping to the floor and stomped on it. "Who cares? I don't give a crap."

She took something else out of her pocket—a penknife. She opened it and began scraping at the stub. Glitter flakes went flying.

"Hey"—I grabbed her wrist, took away the knife—"stop that."

"I don't give a crap," she said again. She pulled the nunchucks from the bedpost. She clacked them together. She smacked her feet down into a karate stance and began swinging the nunchucks around—"Hee-ah! Hee-ah!" Thomas returned then, but when he saw the whirling nunchucks he bolted for the hallway and down the stairs. I had a strong feeling he had been a nunchuck target more than once in his life.

As I watched Alvina twirl and swoop and "Hee-ah!" with her clacking nunchucks, grinning Pooh Bear bouncing on her shoestring necklace, I felt a pang of sadness for her. Maybe I was thinking of my own worst days at Mica High, when I danced but danced alone.

When she finished, she twirled the nunchucks over her

head like a bola and flung them toward the far bedpost. They caught, wrapped around it, and drooped to a stop.

"Impressive," I said. "You practice that?"

"No," she lied.

She fell silent. She kicked the hockey stick. It clattered across the floor and against the wall. She just stood there, staring at it, looking lost, misplaced between her past and future. I wanted to hold her. I wanted to say, *Be patient. You're between two Alvinas. The next one awaits you down the calendar.*

I said, "Alvina . . . there's a man I see down by the stone piles at the old cement plant. He always wears a green watch cap. He always says—"

"'Are you looking for me?'"

"Exactly."

"Crazy Arnold."

"Arnold?"

"Yeah."

"You know him?"

"Everybody knows him. He's wacko." She let out a quick giggle burst. I had never seen her come that close to laughing.

"What?" I said.

She shrugged, the grin gone as fast as it appeared. "Nothin'. Little kids walk behind him and he don't even know it. Then you poke him and say, 'Gotcha!' and he turns around and you scream and run. Just little kids." Abruptly she walked out of the room. "I'm blowing this dump."

On the way out I noticed the inner side of her bedroom door. There was a picture tacked to it, a 3 × 5 school-type color portrait. It was a boy. A blond-haired boy. Where had I seen him? Suddenly it came to me—the Dogwood Festival! It was a picture of the boy she had beaten up. *Good grief*, I thought, *love punches?*

How I wanted to grill her! But I held my tongue (not easy for me, as you know). I finished my gardening, and when Mrs. Klecko came home, I gave her a cleaned-up version of the Great Fingernail Disaster and took Alvina downtown to Lin's Nailery and got her fitted with a new pink, glittery masterpiece.

It wasn't until I got back to my house that I collapsed onto the sofa and finally laughed myself silly at the memory of tiny Thomas mooning his big sister.

July 13

Arnold.

I've been thinking about him. I picture him as a child. Or should I say, a younger child. Little Arnold. Here's what I see: pudgy little kid in a moss-green knit cap with a tassel. Summer. After dinner. Playing with the neighborhood kids down by the cement plant, the stone piles. Playing hide-and-seek. Almost every time they play this game, Little Arnold is the first one to be caught. This time he's determined that won't happen. While the It boy covers his eyes and counts aloud to one hundred, Little Arnold takes off.

This time he doesn't go to the usual places: behind a stone pile, behind the great wheel of a cement truck. This time he runs and he keeps running. Down the railroad tracks and over the canal bridge and down by the river's edge until he can't even hear the It boy counting anymore.

And still he keeps running, along the riverbank, up to the road, along the road—but no, he's in the open, they'll see him, they'll catch him—"Yer It, Arnold!"—so across the farmer's field he goes and back into the trees, running, running, up hills, down hills, his footsteps beating out a tune, *Not this time Not this time*. And finally somewhere near the end of the world he comes to this wonderful hiding place— maybe it's a tunnel into the invisible middle of a thicket of brambles or a woody little nook between two tall stacks of railroad ties—and he squeezes in and settles down and begins to hear the silence beyond his own breathing, and he waits. And thinks, as there's nothing much else to do.

Then a smile comes upon his little round face. Maybe he even giggles—he can't help it—as he thinks of them looking for him, looking for him, looking at each other, saying, "Where's Arnold?" and then—this is the best part—"Arnold's the only one left"—no, *this* is the best part—"Arnold won!" And he waits and thinks and smiles and sometimes he thinks he hears them calling—"Arnold! . . . Arnold!"—and sometimes he thinks they're *right there*, outside the brambles, and sometimes he even flinches because he can *feel* a hand just over his shoulder ready to grab him like they always do as they shout, "Yer It, Arnold!" But they don't . . .

and they don't . . . and the summer bugs are buzzing and somewhere a train whistle calls *Ar-nollllllllld* . . . and when did it get so dark? He holds his hand before his eyes. He cannot find himself.

Sooner or later he comes home—maybe that night, maybe the next day—to frantic parents, police maybe. Life goes on. Games go on. After dinners. Summers. Years. But *that* night, *that* game, that's the one he can't forget, that's the one that never ends.

And I thought, *Arnold knows something that Alvina doesn't know, something that none of the little kids know: he likes it when they poke him from behind and say, "Gotcha!"*

July 18

Another scorcher. It's too hot here! And dry. We've had nine days over 90 degrees in July and hardly any rain. Grass looks like straw. Not even weeds are growing. My Garden Groomer business is hurting.

Today I cooled off at the swim club. I went as a guest of Alvina and her mother. They have a family membership. The three of us jumped in and splashed around for a while. Then Mrs. Klecko and I headed for the shade of the pavilion. It was from there that I looked up and saw someone climbing the chain-link fence that borders the back of the club. He was far away and I couldn't see his face, but I knew instantly it was that boy. Perry. Quick as a monkey, he was up and over the fence, jumping to the ground, popping up from a forward roll, leaping over two sunbathers, and sprinting straight for the pool. He leaped over the NO RUNNING sign into the deep end. He didn't have to change clothes—he was already wearing nothing but ragged, knee-length cutoffs. It must have been ten minutes before I saw him climb out—and before I realized I hadn't taken my eyes off the deep end for a second.

Now he was climbing up the ladder to the high dive. He swaggered out to the end of the board—and just stood there. He was obviously enjoying himself. Not in an arrogant or disdainful way. It was something more like comfort, a sense that he was home, that this was where he truly belonged, poised in his cutoffs at the edge of space, the squealing, splashing multitudes below, glistening in the sun, all the world before him—the King of Pennsylvania.

And then he jumped.

Next time he climbed from the pool a hand reached out and grabbed his ankle and pulled him back in. There were girl screeches and laughing and splashing, and a girl head—red hair—was bobbing next to his, and the two heads kept appearing and disappearing in the sun-spangled water. When they finally emerged it was at the shallow end. The girl wore a pale blue two-piece bathing suit. They flopped onto a brightly colored striped beach towel. The towel was big enough for two, so long as they lay very close to each other.

They were lying there for only a few minutes when

suddenly another girl—it was Alvina—ran toward them from the baby pool and dumped a bucketful of water into Perry's face. She ran off screaming, flinging the bucket, as Perry took off after her. They jumped into the pool, where I lost sight of them. When he emerged, he was alone. He did not return to the girl on the blanket. I don't know why, but this made me a little bit happy.

He jumped again from the high dive. That's when I found myself walking through the sunbathers and squealing children and lowering myself slowly into the water. I waded around. I felt the skin of bodies I brushed by, swatted a volleyball. I paddled underwater, keeping my eyes open for a glimpse of cutoffs. And suddenly there he was, the back of his head popping up in front of me. "Hi!" I said. He turned. I got the impression he didn't recognize me at first, wet hair and all. And then he smiled. And then he dipped his chin into the water and took in a mouthful and spat it into my face, still smiling. And then he was gone. I just stood there, blinking sunwater. A few minutes later I saw him climbing back over the fence and trotting away.

Later, in the pavilion, I said to Alvina, "I saw you with that boy. Perry."

She played with her Pooh Bear necklace. "Yeah. I got him back for taking the donuts from Mrs. Wacko's porch."

"You sure chased him a long way that day."

She was studying her new fingernail. "Did I?"

"I'm surprised you thought a boy was worth chasing that far."

"I woulda smashed his face if I caught him."

"Really?"

"Yeah."

I changed direction. "So I get the impression you know him. Perry."

She shrugged. "I know a lotta people."

"How do you know him?"

"He comes in sometimes."

"You mean to Margie's?"

"Yeah."

"Probably shoplifting donuts, huh?"

"Yeah." She bit one of her nine un-elegant fingernails. "He's a criminal."

"I wouldn't go that far," I said, for some reason wanting to defend him.

"He is," she said. "He was in jail."

Whoa, Nellie!

"Jail?" I said. "Really?"

"Boot camp."

"Boot camp? Army? He's too young."

"It's for kids. It's like the army but it's not. It's for criminal kids. He had to clean toilets with a toothbrush."

"He was sentenced to boot camp?"

"Yeah."

"For what? What did he do?"

"Stealing."

"How long was he in boot camp?"

She shrugged. "I don't know. A year."

I thought of him climbing the fence. Maybe he did that sort of thing on the boot camp obstacle course every day.

"Does he have girlfriends?" Why did *that* pop out?

Her mouth twisted as if she had just bitten into a bug. "How should I know?"

July 19

I'm telling you this, Leo, because:

1. You'll never wind up reading this World's Longest Letter anyway, so it won't make any difference.

Or . . .

2. You will read it, which means you and I would be together, because there's no way I will mail this to you—you may receive it only from my loving hands. Which cannot happen unless we are together in the same room, and I will never again be in the same room with you unless I know that we will be together forever. If that's the case, then, again, it won't make any difference.

So . . .

I missed planting this week's marker at Calendar Hill (that's what I call it now). No, my alarm clock isn't broken. It woke me up on time today. I just never made it out of bed. I had been dreaming. I dreamed I was sitting atop one of the stone piles when Arnold came shuffling by. He was saying something, but it was low and mumbled and I could not understand. I called down, "What did you say?" No answer. He just kept walking. *"Please!"* I called. But he kept walking, and the farther he went, the louder I called. "Please!" At last he came to the canal and jumped in. I ran after him, stood at the edge, peering into the dark waters. I could see a shadow moving, and I knew that it wasn't Arnold anymore, it was someone, or something, else, and I wanted to jump in but I was afraid because I knew that once I entered the water I would drown and become a moving shadow myself.

That's when the alarm went off. I awoke clenched and sweating. I felt relieved and not relieved, because I knew that the dark moving shadow was Perry, and Perry was Ondine and Ondine was Perry, and to prolong a dream moment that was both delicious and dreadful, I chewed time like a wad of bubble gum and stretched it across the darkness all the way to dawn, when the light at the edge of my window told me I was too late to greet the sunrise.

July 23

No dream water today, but real, from the sky: rain! Breaking the heat wave. The grass gave a standing ovation. The flowers cheered.

We were eating Rice Krispies squares in Betty Lou's kitchen—Cinnamon was licking the marshmallow from his own piece—when Dootsie pointed and said, "Night!" We turned to the window. The sky was almost black. Distant rolling rumbles. Lightning flashed white in the kitchen.

(I had a goofy thought: *Did God just take our picture?*) Thunder whacked us. Cinnamon flew into my lap. Dootsie bolted for the back door. I caught her before she got outside.

The violence was over in twenty minutes, but the rain muttered on. Dootsie and I kicked off our shoes and danced in the backyard. We tried to get Cinnamon to dance with us, but he is not fond of water. He scooted under a hydrangea leaf and watched us from there. Betty Lou watched from the screen door. Dootsie and I were holding hands and twirling ourselves dizzy at the end of the yard when Betty Lou shrieked: "Be careful! My night-blooming cereus!" I stopped and looked. The nearest plant rose out of a large, brick-colored clay pot: a gray, woody, spiny vine curling up a broomstick pole. It came up to my shoulder. I remembered that I had first seen it inside the house, by the living room window. "This?" I said.

"Yes. It's my pride and joy. Don't knock into it."

When we came back in, she made us get out of our wet clothes and into bathrobes. Staying inside 24/7 as she does, Betty Lou has lots of bathrobes in her closet. Dootsie looked as if some blue, furry carnivore had swallowed all but her head.

Betty Lou told us about the potted plant:

"It blooms only at night. And only one night each year. That's all. Then it's gone for another year. In fact, mine doesn't even bloom every year. It hasn't bloomed for two years now. See, it's a cactus. It belongs in the desert, not here in Pennsylvania. It misses its home. It comes inside for the winter. My neighbor Mr. Levanthal lugs it in and out for me."

She looked longingly out the window. "My night-blooming cereus." She sighed. "Such a wonderful scent. Like vanilla. It's almost intoxicating. You have to hold on to something or you'll faint from the fragrance."

"What's all that mean?" said Dootsie.

"It means it smells good, honey," said Betty Lou. She looked at me sadly. "It used to be the sweet center of my life. Now it's bittersweet."

I could guess why, but I asked anyway. "How so?"

Another sigh. "I used to be able to tell when it was going to bloom. I would observe the bud closely every day." She chuckled. "I felt like its mother. When I knew it was coming—*tonight!*—I would call the neighbors and we would all gather in the backyard at sunset and have champagne and wait and watch through the night as the petals unfolded and the fragrance filled the air, and we simply stood there as silently as if it were a church and soaked it in, imprinting the rare, fleeting sight in our memories. Sometimes we could actually hear the moths fluttering around us."

"Moths?" I said.

"Oh yes. Many of them. Night-blooming cereus is polli-nated by moths. I believe they, like us humans, are also at-tracted by the fragrance. Or maybe it's the white petals of the flower."

"Only one night," I said.

She nodded. "Only one night. Well before sunrise the petals are already drooping, the blossom is dying."

We didn't speak for a while. The only sound was the *click click* of Cinnamon's hind feet toenails on the tabletop as Dootsie held him upright by his tiny hands, trying to teach him how to dance.

"Ironic," Betty Lou said at last. "The cereus insists on sunlight—that's why it must be at the end of the yard. And yet it saves its flower for the moon. The sun never sees what it fathers."

"It takes from the day," I said, "gives to the night."

She patted my hand. "Very good. You should be a writer." She went to the screen door. The rain had stopped. "Sun's trying to come out," she said. She took a deep breath. "Ahh . . . I'm not so crazy that I can't appreciate a breath of fresh air. Come here, Stargirl." I went to her. "Look at this yard, how drab it is. There used to be an old lady in a ham-burger commercial, she would complain, 'Where's the beef?' Well, I say, 'Where's the flowers?' " She wagged her head for-lornly. "Oh, girls"—she turned and nodded at Cinnamon—"pardon me—oh, girls and *boy*, if only you could have seen my garden before I came inside to stay. It was a showpiece, if I do say so myself. I used to catch people standing at the back fence, looking in. But what's a garden"—she turned away and closed the door—"without a gardener?"

July 25

I saw Arnold ahead of me on the sidewalk today. Two little boys were sneaking up behind him. One reached out and tugged the hem of his peacoat and both yelped, "Gotcha!" and ran. I had this sense that I was watching a play on a stage, that I could come back here day after day and see the same thing. As the boys ran toward me their eyes went buggy with fright—they saw me as a grown-up who was going to holler at them. Just before they got to me they veered off across the street, laughing and pointing at each other: "*He* did it! . . . *He* did it!"

I wanted to call after them: "It's okay! You're just being kids! He's just being Arnold! It's all part of the play!"

July 27

There's a banner across Bridge Street. Blood-red with black trembly letters:

THE BLOB IS COMING!

The Blob is a sci-fi movie from the 1950s. They say it's a cult classic. Part of it was filmed right here at the Colonial Theatre. So every year now they have the Blobfest. No Queens or string bands for this festival. During the day there's a kind of block party downtown—the Blue Comet grills Blob Burgers on the sidewalk—but mostly this is a nighttime event. The townspeople go to the Colonial and watch the original movie. There's no candy or popcorn for sale in the lobby. Instead, Margie sets up shop and hands out Blobbogobs, which are dollops of fried dough that she makes a creepy red with food coloring. The theater is so crowded that people are sitting in the aisles, which makes the fire chief nervous, so the doors are kept open and a fire truck is parked in front of the marquee.

Then they show the movie. The Blob is this alien, dark red glob of goo that lands on earth and terrorizes a small town. It sounds to me—remember, I haven't seen it yet—like the Stomach from Outer Space. It just sort of slimes from place to place and oozes onto people until the people are *inside* of it and it's *digesting* them. I'm told it's actually more funny than disgusting because the special effects in 1958 were not very convincing. But don't tell that to the little kids in the audience, who are screaming away. And because of what's coming, the grown-ups talk themselves into being scared too. Everybody wants to be in the right mood, because what the Blobfest is, more than anything else, is a reenactment.

The climactic scene was filmed in the Colonial Theatre itself—right where the people are sitting. The Blob oozes into the projection room and digests the projection man. Then it starts oozing out through the projection room windows. Somebody in the audience looks up and sees it, and before you know it the whole audience is racing, screaming out of the theater into the street. That's the moment that appears on *Blob* posters all over town—the screamers running from the theater—and that's the scene that the audience a month from now will reenact.

Dootsie told me long ago that I'm taking her. She's already practicing her scream.

July 28

How do you know him?
　He comes in sometimes.
　You mean to Margie's?
　Yeah.

I don't usually go to Margie's on a Saturday. Today I did. He wasn't there.

I listen to the summer symphony outside my window. Truthfully, it's not a symphony at all. There's no tune, no melody, only the same notes over and over. Chirps and tweets and trills and burbles. It's as if the insect orchestra is forever tuning their instruments, forever waiting for the maestro to tap his baton and bring them to order. I, for one, hope the maestro never comes. I love the musical mess of it.

Every day now I stop by Betty Lou's backyard and check the night-blooming cereus. The bud is very long. It reminds me of a giant string bean. It seems fatter, more swollen, with each passing day. And the days are hot and dry again, as if Arizona is visiting. I think of the flower in the bud: huddled, compressed, dark. Yet somehow it feels the night, knows moon from sun. It waits . . . waits.

We never heard the crickets together, Leo. I never saw the moon in your eyes. If you ever kiss me again at night, I'm going to take a peek.

I'm lonely.

July 29

Color now on the end of the bud. White tinged with pink. Feathered, layered, sleeping petals. A miniature swan about to be born.

I groomed two gardens today. I've never seen a night-blooming cereus anywhere but Betty Lou's.

July 31

I hadn't meant to fall asleep. I just flopped onto my bed after dinner, and next thing I knew it was night. The house was dark. I leaped from the bed and ran for my bike. I had told my parents about the flower and that one of these nights . . .

I pedaled furiously for Betty Lou's. The moon was high and bright, lighting my way. My tires spat stones as I careened into the alley. I could smell it already: *vanilla!* I jumped from the bike, threw open the gate. There it was— so lovely I wanted to cry. As if a stone had dropped into pooled moonlight: this was the splash. Its size staggered me— it was as wide as both my hands side by side. I swooned at the fragrance. I fell to my knees, so that now it was taller than me. I became aware of faint flutterings—moths were swirling, alighting on the flower, flying off. I thought: *Queen of the Night*. Kneeling there for I don't know how long, I began to have the strangest sensation, as if a communication, a conversation, were passing between the beautiful blossom and the moon. I closed my eyes and allowed myself to sink into the wonder of it. And yet, as wonderful as it was, something was missing. It needed to be shared. I wanted you there, Leo. Or Archie.

I picked up a handful of pebbles from the alleyway. I threw them at Betty Lou's bedroom window. Finally her face appeared. I pointed. I whispered as loudly as I could: "It's blooming!" Her face vanished from the window. A minute later the back door opened. She stood there in her robe behind the screen door. I held out my hand. "Come on." I think for a moment I forgot her problem. But she didn't.

"I can't," she said.

"It's beautiful," I said.

Her face was moonlit with sadness. "I know."

I held out both hands. "I'm here," I said. "Just for a minute. It'll be all right. You're safe."

"I can smell it from here," she said.

"I know. Yes! Now come see it. It *wants* you to see it."

There were no words for a long time. Then the faint creak of the screen door opening. Her arm reached out, ghostly pale. I took her hand. It would not come with me. "I can't," she said. "I'm sorry." She was crying.

I told her to wait there. I returned to the flower. It took a long time, and I really don't know how I did it, but somehow

I managed to get the great potted plant up the yard to the back door. And that's how we spent the night—Betty Lou and me and the night-blooming cereus. Betty Lou opened a bottle of champagne for herself, as she always did on this occasion, and a cranberry juice for me. The dark screen between us, we toasted the Queen of the Night. We toasted moon and moths and all brief things. We held hands through the opened door and sang soft songs by turns to each other. We shared our dreams. We fell silent as the flower. We fell asleep, she against the screen door, me on the step. When we awoke, the sun was rising and the flower was dead.

August 2

My happy wagon is down to five pebbles.

The temperature today reached 100 degrees. I had a garden job today. I beat the heat by starting early in the morning.

August 3

I awoke in a sweat despite the whirring floor fan at the foot of my bed. I had been dreaming, but already the dream had fled.

I got dressed and tiptoed downstairs. I rode through the night and the high moon, down the middle of empty streets, under the *Blob* banner, to the canal. I crossed the bridge and coasted to a stop in the dust in front of Ike's Bike & Mower Repair. A car was parked out front. I laid the bike down carefully and stood there, listening to the insects. I walked around back. When I saw the ladder I gasped. The roof was only one story high, but it seemed to scrape the moon and felt as forbidding as Babel. I took a deep breath and started climbing.

He was in the middle of the roof, spread-eagled on a blanket, bare-skinned except for the ragged cutoffs he had worn at the pool, sheeted in moonlight. I thought of you, Leo, keeping the shade of your bedroom window up so the moonlight could fall on you. I sat on the raised edge of the roof, watching, listening to his breathing. I think I would have been comfortable staying like that all night—watching, silent—but this was a person, not a backyard flower. At last I called from the edge: "Hi, Perry."

He didn't move.

I tried again, a little louder. "Hi, Perry."

His eyes opened to the sky above. Then they began to move, though the rest of him still did not. They finally landed on me. His head came up several inches from the blanket. His voice was croaky: "Who's that?"

I realized that the moon was behind me now; my face was in shadow. His simple question stumped me. As far as I knew, he didn't even know my name. So how should I identify myself? I thought over several possibilities and finally said, "I'm the girl you spat at."

He laughed, or at least something that resembled laughter

came out of his mouth. His head flopped back down. His eyes closed. I was afraid that was all, but in time he spoke again: "What do you want?"

The questions weren't getting any easier. "Dootsie said you sleep on your roof on hot nights."

"Didn't answer the question." He was right. His voice was straining, its tone saying, *Leave me alone so I can go back to sleep.*

"I guess I don't know what I want," I said. "I woke up. It was hot. I couldn't sleep. I remembered what Dootsie said. And here I am."

"You don't have your own roof?"

"Well, sure, but it's not flat like this. Besides, you're not on my roof. You're on this one."

"You want to sleep *here?*"

"No, no, I don't mean that."

"What do you mean?"

I was very uncomfortable. Whatever had compelled me to come here was gone. "I don't know," I said. "I do things without thinking." I stood. "I'll go. I'm sorry I woke you up."

His hand flapped in the air. "It's okay. I'm awake now." I sat back down. "You got a name?"

"Stargirl," I said. For the first time ever, I felt self-conscious saying it out loud.

His eyes opened. "What?"

"Stargirl."

"*What?*"

I said it for the third time: "Stargirl."

I thought he was going to make a big deal out of it, but he just said, "Okay," and closed his eyes again.

This was such a new script to me. I had no idea what my lines were.

I said, "How can you stand to suck on lemons?"

"Juice is juice," he said.

"Are you going to the Blobfest?"

"Don't know."

"I'm going with Dootsie."

"Good for you."

"You sneak into the pool a lot?"

"When I feel like it."

"You're braver than me. I've never gone off a high dive."

"No big deal."

"It is if you're afraid to do it."

"So you're a coward."

I don't know how I expected things to go, but it wasn't like this. What had made me think I might be welcome? I stood again. "Perry, I really am sorry. I—"

Suddenly he sat up. He snapped: "*You* came over to *my* house and climbed up here and woke *me* up. And now I'm wide awake. Is *that* what you wanted, to wake me up?"

"No," I peeped.

"Well, what *do* you want? You just want to watch me sleep?"

"No."

"You want to talk?"

I was shaking. "I think so."

"So *talk*. You did enough talking before. You follow me home and call me a thief. You lecture me in the library. Who do you think you are, some chief nun or something?"

"No."

"So open your big mouth and *talk*."

I don't know how long I stood there, trying to compose myself. I've never felt so brittle, so defenseless. It was all I could do not to burst out bawling. Until then I hadn't realized what a fragile state I was in.

When I thought I was under control, I did the hardest thing of all: I took a step forward. Then another. The closer I came to him, the clearer it became that the angles were all wrong. I was looming over him. So I sat down, cross-legged, on the warm, papery surface of the roof, about five feet from him. We stared at each other for a long time. In spite of what he had just said, we both seemed to understand that this was not the time to talk. Still staring at him, I reached down and pulled off my sandals and tossed them aside. I think I was making a statement, but I have no idea what it was. Eventually I took a deep breath . . . "I dreamed about you one night."

"Yeah?"

"Well, sort of you. You were swimming in the canal. Dootsie said you do that—"

"Once I did."

"—and I was watching you under the water. You were a dark, shadowy figure, but I knew it was you—and then it wasn't you, it was Ondine, and then you again, and Ondine, back and forth. . . ."

"Ondine," he said.

"The book you were reading in the library that day."

He didn't respond, just stared at me.

"I got my own copy and read it in one sitting. I loved it." He kept staring. "Don't you love it?"

"No."

"Really? Why not?"

"She's stupid."

"How so?"

"She thinks everything is wonderful. Everybody's beautiful."

"Don't you?"

His answer was a snort. "She's always singing. She's too happy."

"Too happy?" I said. "Is that possible? Happy is happy, isn't it? How can you be *too* happy?"

"When you're living in a fairy tale. When the world you're living in is bogus."

"But it's not all peaches and cream for Ondine," I pointed out. "She gets sad."

"Not sad enough. She's stupid. She's not real."

Something suddenly occurred to me. "Perry," I said, edging myself a little closer, "you never finished reading it, did you?"

"It sucked."

"*Did* you?"

"No."

"Well, I have news for you," I said. "In the end Ondine's beloved knight—Hans, remember?—he dies."

"Good."

"And Ondine forgets everything about her time on earth with people and returns to the water."

"Good."

"Forever."

"Good."

The word hung in the night—*good*—like a second, bitter moon.

"So why did you read any of it, then?" I said.

He shrugged. "It was in front of my nose."

He lay back down, his crossed hands a pillow under his head. I was feeling a little more confident now, less uncomfortable, but still he wasn't exactly a bonfire of warmth.

"You know," I said, "this is the second time this week that I've been up all night talking to somebody."

"That so?"

"That's so. And you're dying for me to tell you about the other time, aren't you?"

"Can't wait."

I told him all about the cereus and the night in Betty Lou's backyard. "Betty Lou is the person whose donuts you stole from her porch that day. When Alvina came running after you."

"Who?"

"Alvina Klecko. The girl who chased you. Who dumped the bucket of water on you at the pool."

"The girl with the fingernail."

"That's the one. She says you come into Margie's."

"Once in a while."

"To steal donuts?" My boldness surprised me.

"She gives them to me."

"I think she has a crush on you."

"Sure."

"Really."

"She's a little kid."

"She's a growing kid."

"She's a tomboy."

"She's a tomboy becoming a girl. Look"—I counted off on my fingers—"she gives you donuts. She chased you halfway across town. She threw a bucketful of water on you. That, my dear Perry"—I unfolded one leg and poked him in the knee with my toe—"is love." I quickly withdrew my foot, happy and relieved that he didn't swat it away.

"Alvina told me about boot camp," I said. I looked at him. "Is it okay for me to know?"

He shrugged. "Everybody else does."

His eyes gleamed in the moonlight. I inched closer. I looked at the starry sky. "I don't know what else to ask."

"Try: Why did they send you there?"

"Why *did* they send you there?"

"Stealing."

I had to laugh. "Well, they sure knocked that out of you, didn't they?"

"They tried."

"Was it hard?"

"What?"

"Boot camp. Was it hard on you?"

"Yeah, I guess. Up at four o'clock. Run five miles. Yes, sir. No, sir. Socks on the washline. Classes. Marching. Stand at attention."

"How long? One year?"

"Yeah."

"And still you steal."

He spat across the roof. "Yeah."

I probably shouldn't have prodded him, but I couldn't seem to help myself. "So, what, it's like at the library? If it's in front of your nose, you grab it, right? Book? Donut? Caramel apple? Lemon? Whatever?"

He sniffed. "Nobody gives it to you."

"Aren't you afraid you'll get caught again? Sent back?"

"Nah."

"Maybe you should get a job. Make some money. Then you could—God forbid—pay for things."

"I got plenty of money. I'd rather steal."

Time to change subjects.

"So, are you going to the Blobfest?"

"You asked me that."

"I forget your answer."

"Maybe."

"No maybe for me. Dootsie will drag me if she has to. You going to enter the scary costume contest?"

"Don't think so."

"Dootsie's going to be Mrs. Blob."

"Sounds like a winner."

"Any ideas what I should be?"

"Yourself."

"I'm not scary."

"Don't bet on it."

He didn't crack a grin, but I laughed enough for both of us.

I said, "I meditate."

He said, "I don't."

"Didn't think so. You're not exactly the self-reflective type, are you?"

"Nope."

"Afraid to be alone with yourself?"

"Terrified."

"You seem so sure of everything. Got it all figured out, huh?"

"Yep."

"Tired of all my questions?"

"Not really."

"Do I talk too much?"

"Not for me."

"Really?"

"I like people who talk a lot. Since I don't."

"Well, then"—I threw up my arms—"I'm your girl!"

Now why did I say that?

His eyes opened. He was staring at me. I felt like he was seeing me for the first time. I felt floaty, like a balloon cut loose. I needed to come back down.

"Ask me something," I said.

"Huh?"

"I've been doing all the asking. Now *you* ask *me* a question."

His eyes closed again. "Who dumped you?"

Uh-oh.

"*Dumped* me?"

"Yeah. Who?"

"Where did you hear *that?*"

"Your friend Pootsie."

"Dootsie."

"Dootsie. That day."

"I thought you two were talking about lemonade. I didn't know you were gossiping about me."

"That's all she told me. Your boyfriend dumped you."

Something sweet and sad trickled through me at the sound of his voice calling you my "boyfriend."

"I wouldn't put it that way," I said.

"How would you put it?"

I was afraid he would say that. *Ask me a question*—me and my big mouth.

"Nobody ever said, 'I dump thee. Thou art dumped.' He was under a lot of pressure. It just didn't work out."

"Sorry?"

"Maybe. Sometimes. I don't know."

"What was his name?"

Was that a faint smirk on his lips? He was enjoying this.

"It *wasn't* anything. It *is*."

"Is."

"Leo."

"Where?"

"Arizona. I moved away."

"You loved him."

I said nothing.

"Well?"

"Well what? You just made a statement."

"You loved him? Question mark."

"Of course."

Please don't ask. . . .

"*Love* him? Present tense."

I looked away. The edge of the roof seemed like the edge of the earth. We were on a raft among the stars.

I toe-poked him. "I said ask me *a* question, not twenty questions. Plus, you're too nosy—"

"And you're not?"

"—and I'm not about to tell you every detail of my life on . . ."

"On our first night."

I wasn't going to say that. I wasn't going to say that.

"*Plus*, you're having way too much fun. From now on, *I'll* direct the conversation."

He gave a chuckly sneer. "Typical girl."

"Speaking of girls," I said, "what about the girl at the pool? The one you were lying on the towel with."

"What about her?"

"What's her name?"

"Stephanie."

Stephanie.

"Okay . . . so . . . how about Ike? The bike and lawn mower repairman. Is that your dad?"

"Yeah. What about Stephanie?"

"What does Ike do in the winter? No lawns to mow."

"Snowblowers. What about Stephanie?"

"What about her?"

"Don't you want to know more about her?"

I shrugged. "Not really."

"Is she my girlfriend? Do I like her? Do I love her? Are we getting married? How many kids are we gonna have?"

He was smirking again.

"Funny," I said. "I have a better idea. Let's talk about my calendar. Bet you didn't know I'm making a calendar."

"Congratulations."

"It's not the kind you're thinking."

"What am I thinking?"

"The paper kind. You hang it on a wall."

"You read my mind. How'd you get so smart?"

"I'm ignoring your sarcasm. My calendar is from before there was such a thing as paper. Ever hear of the Solstice?"

He let out a long, bored breath. "Winter or Summer?"

Surprise, surprise. "Winter."

"When the sun is over the Tropic of Capricorn. Shortest day of the year."

I think I just blinked and gawked at him for a while. He appeared to have gone off to sleep.

"Am I boring you?"

"Nope."

I'm not sure I believed him, but I went on and told him about my weekly work at Calendar Hill. "I'm aiming for December twenty-first, as of course you well know, Solstice expert that you are. I want to have a kind of—I don't know—ceremony? Celebration? I want to give it a name. Got any ideas?"

A pause for five seconds, and he said, "Solstar."

"Huh?"

"Solstar. *Star*-girl. *Sol*-stice. Reversed."

I was overcome. Silly, I know—it was such a small thing. But hearing him say my name for the first time, a kind of thrill went through me. He was not as indifferent to me, not as bored, as he appeared.

I cleared my throat. "I like it. Thank you."

"You're welcome."

"So," I went on, "I'm going to have a tent, with a hole in it, exactly in line with the last spatula, pointing to the horizon, ready to funnel the first rays of the rising sun into my tent. A kind of tenty Stonehenge. I'm going to invite people."

I waited for him to ask me why I was doing all this. He didn't.

"It's going to be the neatest moment," I said. "Maybe I'll write a poem. Or a song. I could play my ukulele. I could dance." I got up. I danced. I danced out to the edges of the roof, where I could see the canal silvery in the moonlight. I danced a circle around him. When I was behind him, he did not turn to watch me, but he did sit up. When I sat back down, he said nothing. He looked at me and nodded.

"So," I said, "maybe you could come with me some morning when I go to plant a new marker."

"Maybe."

"Or meet me there. I go on Thursdays."

"Maybe."

My sense is that after the second "maybe" we looked at each other for hours, but I guess it could have been only minutes, maybe less. Roof time is harder to track than sunrise time. Sooner or later I said, "Well . . ." I put on my sandals and stood. "'Night."

"'Night," he said.

I went to the edge. He was lying back down. "And I am *not* a typical girl," I said, and I stepped onto the ladder and returned to earth.

August 8

A mockingbird has moved into our neighborhood. It perches atop a telephone pole behind our backyard. Every morning it is the first thing I hear. It is impossible to be unhappy when listening to a mockingbird. So stuffed with songs is it, it can't seem to make up its mind which to sing first, so it sings them all, a dozen different songs at once, in a dozen different voices. On and on it sings without a pause, so peppy, frantic even, as if its voice alone is keeping the world awake.

August 9

Before I walked to Calendar Hill today, I asked my mother about our next-door neighbors, the Cantellos, and their porch light. I notice that it's on every time I go to the hill. At first I had thought they left it on by mistake, but now I was beginning to wonder. "It's no mistake," my mother said. She said she told Mrs. Cantello about my Thursday early-morning ritual, so now Mrs. Cantello helps to light the way for me. Isn't that nice?

August 10

I told Betty Lou about the rooftop night with Perry.

"What about Leo?" she said. (I had long since told her about you.)

"Leo's there," I said. "Perry's here."

I also told Betty Lou about the mockingbird. "You're so lucky," she said. "I wish I had a mockingbird."

August 11

Dear Archie,

(Letter within a letter here, Leo, but you're allowed to peek—as I said before, I have nothing to hide from you.)

I met a boy. Perry. I don't even know his last name. He lives behind a bike and lawn mower repair shop. (Remember what lawn mowers are, you desert dweller?) He has dark hair, blue eyes. Sometimes he sleeps on the roof. He seems to be poor. He scavenges in Dumpsters. He steals. He's been in trouble with the law. He went to one of those so-called boot camps for a year. He sucks on lemons. He spits the seeds at me. He doesn't talk much (though he did holler at me once). He's often grumpy. But he was nice to my little friend Dootsie. Maybe the best thing I can say about him is that Dootsie really seems to like him. He reads. He introduced me to *Ondine*. He's very smart, but it takes a while to find that out. Sometimes he acts as if he owns the world. He swaggers. When he climbs the ladder to the high dive at the pool, he doesn't jump right off but stands there for a while, surveying his domain. He lay on a beach towel with a girl named Stephanie, but after he went in the water he didn't return to her. My friend Alvina the Pip has a crush on him.

"Do *you?*" I hear you say.

I don't know, Archie. I have *something*, but I don't know what to call it. I spent almost a whole night on his roof with him (no hanky-panky). We talked . . . well, I talked mostly (except when he hollered at me). I danced for him. He gives so little that all he needs to do to make me feel good is to keep his eyes open.

"What about Leo?"

You're not the first to ask me that. At the moment I must admit I'm just not thinking a whole lot about Leo. In fact, I'm deliberately *not* thinking about him. Every day when I wake up, the question is there waiting for me: *What about Leo?* But I turn away from it. I pretend I don't hear. Do you think it's because I'm afraid of the answer? I wish Dootsie could meet Leo in person. As it stands, she despises him because he "dumped" me.

If this were happening in Mica, I'd be sitting on your porch about now, you and me on the white rockers, you puffing away on your pipe, the air smelling like cherries. You would listen and you would nod and smile and patiently wait until I was finished talking. You'd ask a few questions. Then you might say, "Why don't we go consult Señor Saguaro?" And we would walk over to the Señor and you would speak to him in Spanish and he would answer and you would translate for me, and between the two of you— you and Señor Saguaro—you would make things a little clearer for me, you would show me the way.

Your Pupil, Loving and Forever,
Stargirl

August 14

Today was Charlie's birthday. It says so on the tombstone he shares with Grace. August 14, 1933. Then the dash. Then the blank space, patiently waiting. I had been thinking of today for some time. I had gotten Charlie a gift. I wrapped it. White paper, blue ribbon.

I had decided that today would be the day I would walk right up to Charlie and say something.

I was about to head for the cemetery when Dootsie came bursting in: "Let's go someplace!"

Dilemma.

On one hand, just the day before, my father had worked up a little pull cart for my bike, so I could haul Dootsie along when I took it out. Dootsie was rabid for a ride. On the other hand, it would be all I could do to fight off my terror and face Charlie—how could I manage Dootsie and her unpredictability at the same time? On the third hand, how could I say no to that begging little face beaming up at me?

"Okay," I said, and before she stopped squealing, I had the new cart hitched up and we were rolling. Cinnamon sat in Dootsie's lap. Along the way I tried to explain the situation as best I could. I told her that Charlie was sad because he missed his wife, and he came here every day. I told her that we must respect his feelings and not bother him. I was simply going to give him the gift and maybe say a brief something, and then we would go. Dootsie was to stand by me and not say a word. Usually I rode my bike into the cemetery. This time I parked at the entrance. I put Cinnamon in my pocket. As Dootsie climbed from her cart, I knelt in front of her, held her by the shoulders, and looked her in the eye. "Do you understand all that now?"

She nodded vigorously. "Yep," she said. "And I'm *not* gonna say a word." To prove it, she locked her lips and threw away the key.

We headed for the grave site. Dootsie pointed. She whispered, "Is that Charlie?"

"Yes," I whispered, "now *shhh*."

We approached him from the side. If he could see us out of the corner of his eye, he didn't show it. My kneecaps were Jell-O. If Dootsie hadn't been there, I think I would have turned and run. I kept telling myself: *He accepted your donuts. He's only a man. He won't bite you.* I also kept hearing Perry's voice: *Who do you think you are?*

As always, he sat in the aluminum chair with green and white strapping. He wore a white short-sleeved shirt, black pants and shoes, white socks. His shins were almost as white as his socks. The old black lunch pail sat in the grass. The red and yellow plaid scarf was draped across his thigh. For the first time it struck me that that was all. No magazine, no book, no portable radio or TV, no headphones—nothing else to "do," nothing else to help him pass the time. Even in death, Grace was all he needed. In his own way, he was echoing the legend of the Lenape girl. He had already leaped—it was just taking him longer to fall.

We stopped a few feet away. Still, he didn't seem to

know we were there. Dootsie's tiny hand was wrapped around my finger. When I finally dared to look directly at his face, I discovered to my horror that he was faintly smiling. No doubt he was reliving a happy moment with Grace or maybe having a conversation with her. I was mortified. *You idiot! You busybody! Get out! Leave the man in peace! Run!* And I might have, had he not suddenly turned his head and looked up at us. For the first time I was fully seeing the face that Grace had lived with. The smile was gone. His eyes, out from under the shade of the cap brim, were looking at us from another place. Grief had not pared him down. He was beefy. His wrists were thick as hoagie rolls, his arms blotchy and red and white-haired from the summer's sun. There was a thready logo above the pocket of his white shirt. It said GOSHEN GEAR WORKS.

"I'm sorry—" I stammered. "I—" I didn't have a clue what to say.

All of a sudden Dootsie snatched the gift from me, thrust it out to him, and piped, "Happy birthday, Charlie!"

I just stood there like a dunce while Dootsie took over. When Charlie failed to take the gift, Dootsie laid it in his lap. He didn't take his eyes off her. Dootsie didn't wait very long before saying, "Aren'tcha gonna open it?" She didn't wait for an answer. She grabbed it and tore off the paper and ripped open the box. She took it out. "Look!"

He looked at the gift, at her, at me. "It's a mister," I said. "You spray it on yourself to keep cool in the hot weather."

Dootsie shook the plastic bottle. "Look—we already filled

it with water. Want me to spray you?" She took his non-reply for a yes. She sprayed one of his forearms. Droplets glistened like dew on the freckled white meadow of hair. He kept staring at his arm. At last he reached out. He took the mister from her hand. He sprayed his other arm. Dootsie snatched the bottle back. She sprayed her own face. Then mine. Then *his*. He blinked. She yelped, "Yes!" and jumped up and down and twirled around and sprinted twice around the tombstone and handed the mister back to him. Still he had not cracked a smile, but his eyes were different now, they were *here*.

Dootsie propped herself in front of him. "So, Charlie, how old are you today?"

Charlie showed her with fingers. Dootsie counted them up. "*Eleven?*"

"Seventy-four," I said. At first I thought it was cute, answering the little girl's number question with fingers; then something else occurred to me.

"I'm six," Dootsie was saying. "Stargirl is sixteen. She got dumped."

He was looking a little confused. I was looking a little miffed.

I stepped in front of him and waited for him to look up at me. I pointed to my ear and enunciated as clearly as I could, "Can you hear?"

He shook his head no.

I put my hand on Dootsie's shoulder. "Charlie can't hear you."

Dootsie cupped her hands around her mouth, and before I could stop her she bellowed full into his face, "CAN? YOU? HEAR? ME?"

He looked up at me. He was smiling. I thought: *We're sharing something! Two grown-ups smiling over the antics of a little kid.* Then he was reaching into a pocket and pulling out a pinkish thingy and putting it in his ear. He leaned in to Dootsie's face. "Now I can hear you."

Nosy me, I asked him, "Why weren't you wearing it?"

"I don't never wear it here," he said. "So I can hear Grace better."

His voice was gruff, callused like his meaty hands.

Dootsie looked at me, at him. "Is Grace your wife who died?"

He nodded.

"And you're sad because she died, aren't you?"

He nodded.

She said, "I'll be sad with you, Charlie." She climbed onto his lap and hugged him. He closed his eyes and stroked her hair. I stared at the tombstone.

When she climbed down from his lap, she propped her elbows on his knees and said, "Are you going to the Blob Festibal?"

He shook his head. "No."

"I am," she said brightly. "I'm going as Mrs. Blob. I'm going to win!"

He looked at me. "Mrs. Blob?"

I shrugged. "Her idea." I tapped Dootsie. "Okay, young

lady, time to go. We've bothered Charlie enough for one day." I pulled her to her feet.

She stuck out her arm. "Nice to meet you, Charlie." Before he could respond she cried out, "Wait! I forgot!" She pulled Cinnamon from my pocket. She held him in front of Charlie's face. She held out Cinnamon's tiny paw. "You have to meet Cimmamum."

Charlie didn't bat an eyelash. He took Cinnamon's tiny paw between his thumb and forefinger and shook it. Dootsie tugged at him till he bent over. She sat Cinnamon on his shoulder. He straightened up. He and Cinnamon looked at each other. He turned to the gravestone and—proudly, it seemed to me—posed for Grace.

"Well . . . ," I said at last, not trusting myself to say more. I returned Cinnamon to my pocket.

Dootsie grabbed Charlie's hand and shook it. "Goodbye, Charlie." She waved at the tombstone. "Goodbye, Mrs. Charlie."

"Goodbye—" said Charlie, and looked at me, frowning.

"She's Dootsie," I said.

The frown stayed.

Dootsie said it this time, tugging him back down to her: *"Doot-sie."*

He nodded.

"Say it," she said.

He almost grinned. "Dootsie."

I led her away, then heard him call, "Hey." I turned. "You?"

"Stargirl." I saw the puzzled look. "Really," I said.

He smiled. "Funny names, you two."

We continued walking and he called again: "Hey." I turned. "The donuts." He pointed. "You?"

I nodded. "Me."

He didn't actually say the words "thank you." He didn't have to.

As I climbed onto my bike, I wondered why in the world I ever hesitated to bring Dootsie along.

August 16

Thursday. The one day in the week I'm up earlier than the mockingbird. Today I was up earlier than usual. I pretended my mother didn't notice.

I go on Thursdays.

I had said that to him on the roof. Was I just giving information? Or more?

I practically ran to Calendar Hill.

He wasn't there.

Why should he be? I hadn't flat-out asked him to come (dummy).

I walked about the field. I joined the singing insects. The moon rose higher and higher. Was the moon looking for him too? I scanned the horizon for shadows. I walked about with the flashlight on, so I couldn't be missed by anyone nearby. When the sun arrived I planted the new marker and went home.

August 18

I did errands downtown for Betty Lou today. I was in the dollar store, paying for lightbulbs and hairpins at the checkout counter, when I looked out the window and saw Perry across the street. With a girl. Ponytail. Not red-haired Stephanie. Ponytail was holding something out to him. He took a bite of it. She playfully kicked him in the behind. He playfully kicked her. They laughed and jostled on up the street.

Suddenly I had to talk to Alvina. Now. I ran to Margie's.

"Alvina in?" I said, breathless.

Margie thumbed over her shoulder. "Back."

I almost cheered. I pushed through the swinging door. Alvina was cleaning donut trays.

I had my first question ready—my life could not proceed without the answer—but I didn't want to be too obvious. I started out with everyday chitchat, waiting for an opening. When it came, I tried to sound as if it had just occurred to me: "Oh yeah . . . remember that guy? Perry? What's his last name, anyway?"

She snapped donut crumbs from a rag. "Delloplane," she said.

Ah, Perry Delloplane. "You think he's cute?" Where did *that* come from? I hadn't planned to say that.

Alvina was giving me and my question an I-smell-a-skunk face when Margie's voice came roaring from out front: "Alvina!"

A customer had spilled a MargieMocha all over the floor, and Alvina had to mop it up. Then she had to take over the counter while Margie went to the bathroom. One thing after another occupied Alvina for the next hour, so I finally gave up and left.

I am a mess. Like that MargieMocha, I am spilled across a floor, but there's nobody to mop me up. I have only one thing to show for the day: *Perry Delloplane*. The sound of a name. It is a grape in my mouth. I roll it over and over on my tongue—*perrydelloplaneperrydelloplaneperrydelloplaneperrydelloplane*—but when I try to crush it with my teeth, it slips away.

August 19

Today the mockingbird doesn't sound happy. It sounds as if it's coming apart. As if the very heart of itself—its song—is breaking into pieces and flying off in a hundred directions.

August 21

I do my job. I weed the gardens of other people. I pull out the weeds and put them in plastic bags and the people throw them out with the trash. When I am finished there is nothing left but flowers and other proper, upstanding not-weeds. I sometimes almost hear the flowers say to me,

Ah . . . thank you for getting rid of that riffraff. It was junking up the neighborhood. I've become pretty good at telling weeds from not-weeds. But every once in a while I have my doubts. I come across an especially difficult root. I pull and it doesn't come out. I pull again. It resists. I dig my gloved fingers into the soil and grab it with both hands and pull yet again. It begins to come out, but I can see it's going to take several more hard pulls. And that's when the doubts begin. I begin to wonder: *Have I made a mistake? Is this really a weed? If it's not supposed to be here, why is it resisting so?* But it's too late now. There's nothing to do with a plant half pulled but to go all the way. And so I tug some more, and finally, shedding clods of dirt and worms, it breaks free of the earth—and I try not to hear the tiny, anguished cry.

August 23

Another Thursday morning on Calendar Hill. By myself.

A TV crew came to Bridge Street today. They were filming the *Blob* banner and the front of the Colonial Theatre. They interviewed the mayor, who said, "It was our lucky day when *The Blob* crawled into town."

My mother talked me out of dressing up Cinnamon and taking him as Frankenrat. She pointed out that in a crowd like that, someone might panic at the sight of a rat. It might not be safe for Cinnamon.

No such problem with Dootsie. My mother was so pleased with the Mrs. Blob outfit that she came with me to deliver it. The moment Dootsie saw it she put it on—which was pretty easy, since all she had to do was lower it over her whole self. No arms, no legs to deal with. My mother had sewn together a couple of sheets, dyed pink, and stitched clumps of cushion foam throughout the space between. The result was a pink, lumpy, formless droop—a Blob—that reminded me of a giant, rumpled sock. There were two eye-holes and, lest anyone mistake the Mrs. for a Mr., a cute little thimble-shaped hat. The droop was purposely made much too long, so that the hem crumpled about her feet and oozed across the floor. Mrs. Blob looked as if she were sprouting wings as two hidden arms punched upward and she declared, "I'm a winner!" Then she came sliming after us—and we ran screaming from the house.

August 24

By 6 p.m. Bridge Street was mobbed with Blobs and other assorted despicables, as all monsters were eligible for the contest. Demons, witches, zombies, skeletons, aliens, phantoms, ghouls, cannibals—and Blobs—all came slogging down the sidewalks toward the Colonial Theatre.

The theater lobby was Monstrosity Grand Central. I spotted a blood-splattered hag with one elegant fingernail.

She was accompanied by a short Frankenstein and a man I assumed to be Mr. Klecko. I spotted the ponytailed girl I had seen Perry with. And red-haired Stephanie from the pool. But no Perry.

Everyone was reaching for Margie's fried dough Blobogobs. This was where Dootsie ran into a snag. Because my mother had not given the costume a mouth hole ("The Blob doesn't *have* a mouth," she said, "the Blob *is* a mouth"), I had to feed Dootsie her Blobbogob through an eyehole.

When the last seat in the balcony was filled, the monsters were invited backstage. One by one they came out from behind the curtain and crossed the stage to the hoots and whistles of the crowd. Dootsie started out well—she even got a few wolf whistles. Then she had problems. She tripped over her hem and fell. When she got up, she felt for her hat and discovered it wasn't on her head, it was still on the floor, but she didn't know exactly where because her eyeholes were now at the back of her head and she couldn't see. She was crawling blindly around the floor, feeling for her hat—*really* looking like a Blob now—and crawled right off the edge of the stage. I jumped up and yelled, "Dootsie!"— but a judge was there, catching her. He put her back, stood her up, replaced her hat, and pulled her eyeholes around to her eyes. She hiked her sheet up to her neck, showing the world she wore nothing else but her Babar the Elephant underpants, and ran off the stage to laughter and the loudest ovation of the night.

There were two sections: little kids and big kids. The little-kid winner was . . . "Dootsie Pringle!" Among the big kids, Alvina got an honorable mention. I wished Betty Lou were there to see it all.

When the monsters were back in their seats, the lights went down and the movie began. What I had heard about the movie was true—it's more funny than scary, at least to the older kids and the adults in the audience. But that didn't stop the little kids from screaming every time the Blob oozed across the screen. The big scene came over an hour into the film: the Blob oozing out of the projection booth, the audience screaming, stampeding under the marquee and into the street— The film suddenly stopped, freezing the fleeing figures in mid-scream, calf-length skirts and pompadours flying. The theater lights went on. A basso voice came over the PA: "Okay, Blobbonians, this is the moment you've been waiting for. The most famous moment in horror movie history—and it took place rrrrright here, in *yyyour* Colonial Theatre. Now is your chance to relive that history. Finish your Blobbogobs, spritz up your vocal cords, and get rrrrrready to scream, Blobbonians. And remember—parents, hold on to your children. Nobody gets trampled. Nobody gets hurt. This is civilized bedlam. One row at a time. Starting at the back. Last row first. Slow and easy does it into the lobby—and then out the door and . . . *lllllllllet 'er rip!* The cameras are rolling. Back row, get going . . . NNNNNOW!"

We weren't supposed to act terrified until we hit the

sidewalk, but as soon as the announcer said "NNNNNOW!" every little kid screamed. The rows funneled into the aisles. We were in one of the front rows, so by the time we reached the lobby the bedlam from outside was backwashing over us, and for the first time in my life I felt the force of a stampeding mob. Afraid for Dootsie, I started to lift her, but she broke away from me and plunged into the crowd, waving her arms inside her pink sheet, shoving aside other little kids in her panic to escape the creeping goo, tripping over the sheet, falling on her face, getting up, the mob trampling her thimble hat. I lost sight of her, then spotted her as we were swept through the doors and into the screaming blaze of the marquee and TV lights. I grabbed the top of her and a moment later had nothing but a pink sheet in my hand as she ran screaming down the middle of Bridge Street, naked except for her sneakers and Babar the Elephant undies.

I caught her at the traffic light. She was laughing and yelling: "I'm ternified!" I wrapped the sheet around her till she looked like a tiny Roman with a sloppy toga. We joined the after-panic crowd milling outside the theater. Many were going back in to watch the rest of the movie. We were about to join them when Dootsie shouted: "Perry!" She broke from me and ran to Pizza Dee-Lite, directly across the street from the Colonial. Perry was sitting at a table at the front window, watching the festivities. Red-haired Stephanie sat across from him.

I watched as Dootsie burst into the restaurant and announced, "I won!" and leaped into Perry's lap. Stephanie laughed. A two-pronged fork of jealousy stabbed deep into me.

Dootsie was jabbering in Perry's face as I walked in. Perry looked past her ear and gave me a smile and turned to Stephanie. "This is her," he said.

This is her.

Stephanie looked up at me. Her red hair was especially bright in the fluorescent light. She pulled a string of cheese from her chin and fed it into her mouth. She wiped her fingertips on a napkin and jabbed her hand out to me. Her smile looked unforced. "It's really Stargirl? Your name?"

I shook her hand. "Really," I said.

"Homeschool, huh?"

"Yes."

She wagged her head. "Too bad."

"How's that?" I said.

"We could use you at the high school. We need some *fascinating* people there." She flung the word "fascinating" across the table at Perry, her eyes flaring for an instant. She turned back to me, smiled. "We already have enough boring ones."

Perry said, "I didn't say 'fascinating.'"

She pistol-pointed at him. "That's right. He said you were weird." She chuckled and picked a pepperoni disk from her slice and pitched it across the table. Perry caught it in his mouth. It could not have been done so neatly without a lot of practice. "I'd hit him if I were you."

"I told her you were interesting," Perry said to me.

Dootsie wanted attention. She rose up on Perry's lap. She grabbed him by the ears and swung his face to hers. "I'm *telling* you how I won."

The word "interesting" fluttered about my head.

"Sit," said Stephanie.

I sat. I felt like I was auditioning.

A blood-splattered hag appeared at the table. "Hello, Alvina," I said, but she was focused only on Perry. Perry had just picked up a slice of pizza and was about to chomp into it when Alvina snatched it from his hand. "Yo," he said, "take that one." He pointed to the last piece on the platter. "I want this one," she said, and bit into it.

"She beats up boys," Dootsie told Perry.

Alvina took the last empty chair.

"Congratulations on your honorable mention," I said.

"I stunk," she said.

"I won!" said Dootsie.

"Where are your parents?" I asked Alvina.

"They went home."

"Out alone at night," said Stephanie. "Big girl."

Dootsie piped, "She *is* a big girl. Look." She grabbed Alvina's little finger and displayed the fancy fingernail.

Stephanie whistled. "Impressive."

Dootsie reached across the table and plucked the last pepperoni disk from Stephanie's slice. "Open," she commanded Perry, and from a distance of one inch she tossed it into his mouth.

Alvina picked a pepperoni from her own slice and

pitched. She missed. Dootsie picked the piece from Perry's lap and handed it back to Alvina. This time Alvina held the piece out to Perry's lips. He took it between his teeth. He tugged. She held it for a second, then let it go. I wondered if he still believed she didn't have a crush on him.

"Looks like I'm the only girl at the table who hasn't fed Perry tonight," I said.

Then a voice behind me: "Hi."

It was Ponytail. With a zombie.

"Ooh, yum," said Ponytail. She grabbed the last slice and took a big bite. "How'd you know I wanted pepperoni?"

Zombie snatched the slice from Ponytail, folded it, and stuffed the whole thing into her mouth. She said something that came out: "Yuh yuh yuh yuh."

All the girls started laughing and swatting playfully at each other. There didn't seem to be any animosity among them. Suddenly Zombie leaned in to Perry and gave him a long kiss on the lips. Dootsie folded her arms and glared at the smoochers. Alvina looked the other way, as if the chair beside her were empty. She pretended to be searching for someone in the restaurant. Finally, while the kiss was still going on, she popped up and left. I wished I could have too. Zombie somehow managed to take Alvina's vacated seat while continuing to kiss Perry. Finally Dootsie snarled, "That's e-*nuff*," and pushed Zombie's face away.

More laughter.

"Who's the little chick?" said Ponytail.

"Miss Dootsie Pringle," I said.

"I'm not a little chick," said Dootsie. "I'm Mrs. Blob."

Perry gestured toward me. "And this is Stargirl."

"I thought so," said Ponytail. "Cool name."

"Thanks," I said.

"Your parents name you that?"

"I did."

"And it's okay with them?"

"Sure."

"Cool parents. Your mother homeschools you, huh?"

Was there anyone Perry hadn't blabbed to?

"Yes," I said.

"Cool. Did you ever go to real school?"

"Homeschool *is* real school," Perry said.

She stuck her tongue out at Perry, then turned a friendlier face to me. "You know what I mean."

I nodded. "I know. Yes. I went to a regular high school last year."

"Yeah? Where?"

"Arizona."

The girls boggled. "Really?" said Stephanie. "What was that like?"

"Hot."

Zombie snickered. "You mean the guys?"

I thought: *One guy.*

I said, "I mean the weather."

"Didn't like it?" said Ponytail. "That why you're back to homeschooling?"

"It didn't go as well as I had expected," I said.

Zombie said, "But don't you miss, like, the people? Other kids?"

"I'm with people a lot," I said.

"*I'm* a people," said Dootsie. "I'm a human bean." She clamped Perry's nose between her fingers and twisted hard.

Perry yelped: "Oww!"

Dootsie wagged her finger in his face. "Don't let me catch you kissing any more girls."

Zombie smirked. "That'll be the day."

"Looks like you have a new girlfriend," said Stephanie. Then she turned to me, but she didn't speak. She just looked at me. She seemed faintly amused. Finally she said, "So. Stargirl. What do you think?"

Everyone's eyes were on me.

"Think about what?" I said.

"About joining Perry's harem?"

I don't know how long I sat there looking like a doofus before Dootsie finally rescued me. "What's a harem?" she said.

Ponytail, the only one left standing, reached down and button-pressed Dootsie's nose. "A harem is when a bunch of girls all like the same guy."

Zombie stuck her finger in Perry's ear. "Even if the guy's a wing nut."

Ponytail laid a hand on my shoulder. "Little Perry over there doesn't want to get serious about anybody—"

"—so he's semi-serious about a bunch of us," said Stephanie.

"Perry's a rolling stone," said Zombie. "He belongs to nobody. Right, Per?"

Perry kept his usual stone face, but I could tell he was enjoying all this. The winky looks I was getting from the girls made me wonder if he had told them about our night on the roof. I hoped not.

Zombie poked him. "Tell her your nickname, Per."

Perry sniffed. "You tell her."

She grinned. "Dandy."

I looked at Perry. "Dandy?"

"As in dandelion," said Zombie.

"As in flower," said Ponytail. "As in a flower that attracts lots of honeybees." She looked at the others, grinning. "And we are—ta-da!" Each of the three girls hoisted a leg onto the table to show nickel-size black and yellow tattoos of honeybees on their ankles. They looked fake, the wash-off type. I hoped they were.

"And Dandy"—Zombie pinched his cheek—"is the flower."

Ponytail snapped her fingers. "Hey—" She pointed at me. "*Stargirl*—" She pointed at herself and the others. "We could be . . . *Perry*girls!"

Stephanie and Zombie did a drumroll on the tabletop. "Yes!"

Stephanie was staring at me. "She thinks we're kidding."

Ponytail studied me. "She thinks we're lying."

Zombie poked Perry. "Are we lying, Dandy?"

Perry looked at me. He nodded. "They're lying."

"*I* lie," said Dootsie, but her confession was lost in the laughter and playful battering Perry took from the three girls.

"There's only one thing about Perry Delloplane that's a lie," said Stephanie.

I took the bait. "What's that?"

"He didn't really go to boot camp. He went to—" She looked at the others and swept her arms like an orchestra conductor, and on the downbeat they all belted out, "BOOTY CAMP!" and laughed and slapped hands.

Dootsie was fed up with being ignored, and now she saw her opening. She climbed onto the table and stood on the empty aluminum pizza platter. "*I* got a booty!" she proclaimed to everyone, and she hiked up her toga and started to wiggle and a dozen tiny gray Babars shimmied in our faces. Whistles and catcalls flew across the restaurant.

I stood. "Okay. That's it." I lifted her from the table. She protested. So did the girls. "It's past your bedtime," I told her. "Your parents are going to kill me."

Patrons applauded as I carried her off. As we went out the door, she called back over my shoulder: "I won!"

On our way up Bridge Street we passed a Laundromat. A lady was sitting inside, reading a magazine. In front of her, two dryers were running. Behind the portholes clothes were tumbling . . . tumbling . . .

Like me.

August 25

The mockingbird does not dump me. The mockingbird has no harem. The mockingbird takes nothing, demands nothing. The mockingbird does nothing but give—give its song. After listening to the mockingbird all day, I feel Mockingbird is now my second language. I offer here the world's first Mockingbird-to-English translation, as recorded late this afternoon:

"Ha ha ho ho hee hee! Wait'll you hear this one. Beep! Beep! I feel like crooning. Bah bah bah bah boo! Barry Manilow, eat your heart out. Hey hey the gang's all here! Ha ha ho ho hee hee! Don'tcha just love me? Hey hey the gang's—hey, where's the gang? Who needs 'em anyway. Babababababaaaaa babababababooooo. Hey, I just heard a cat-bird the other day. Check this out: meow meow. Nailed it, didn't I? Carnegie Hall, eat your heart out. Heeheehaha-hoho. And now, ladies and germs, my impression of a cow-bird: Meowmoo! Meowmoo! Thank you thank you. No need to stand when you applaud. Don'tcha just love me? Hotcha hotcha hotcha!"

August 29

First day of school. I'm now a retired gardener. And Dootsie starts first grade. I hope her teacher got a lot of rest over the summer.

The public school kids will have just a half day. Not this homeschooler. My mother doesn't believe in half days. "You either have a day or you don't," she says. "Is education so scary they feel they have to sneak up on it? Doesn't it bother anybody to cut time in half?"

I guess all this led her to my first assignment of the new school year . . .

FIELD TRIP:
THE CLOCK ON THE MORNING LENAPE BUILDING
Must clocks be circles?
Time is not a circle.
Suppose the Mother of All Minutes started
right here, on the sidewalk
in front of the Morning Lenape Building, and the parade
of minutes that followed—each of them, say, one inch long—
headed out that way, down Bridge Street.
Where would *Now* be? *This* minute?
Out past the moon?
Jupiter?
The nearest star?

Who came up with minutes, anyway?
Who needs them?
Name one good thing a minute's ever done.
They shorten fun and measure misery.
Get rid of them, I say.

Down with minutes!
And while you're at it—take hours
with you too. Don't get me started
on them.

Clocks—that's the problem.
Every clock is a nest of minutes and hours.
Clocks strap us into their shape.
Instead of heading for the nearest star, all we do
is corkscrew.
Clocks lock us into minutes, make Ferris wheel
riders of us all, lug us round and round
from number to number,
dice the time of our lives into tiny bits
until the bits are all we know
and the only question we care to ask is
"What time is it?"

As if minutes could tell.
As if Arnold could look up at this clock on
the Lenape Building and read:
15 Minutes till Found.
As if Charlie's time is not forever stuck
on Half Past Grace.
As if a swarm of stinging minutes waits for Betty Lou
to step outside.
As if love does not tell all the time the Huffelmeyers
need to know.

My mother raved over it. She put it on the refrigerator. "Wait," she said, and left. She came back with her wristwatch and a hammer. We went out back. "You want to do it?" she said.

"Okay," I said.

I laid the watch on the bottom step. I hit it with the hammer. The crystal cracked, that was all.

"Here," she said, taking the hammer from me. She wound up like Paul Bunyan and down came the hammer and to pieces went the watch. Minutes flew off like fleas.

I did the same to my watch. We got a garden trowel and buried the pieces. We took down all the clocks in the house and dumped them in the trash.

"I don't have to tear down Calendar Hill, do I?" I said.

"No," she said. "That's real time."

August 30

Two more porch lights have joined the Cantellos' along the way to Calendar Hill. Curious.

September 1

I sliced an orange in half.

In the back of our backyard sits a barbecue pit. It came with the house. We haven't used it yet. It's made of brick. The top row of bricks is almost as high as me. That's where I placed an orange half, sliced side up.

September 3

Margie herself was sweeping the floor today.

"Where's Alvina?" I asked her.

She leaned on the broom, sighed, wagged her head. "I fired her."

(Can you be "fired" from a job that pays you in donuts?)

"What happened?" I said.

"Fighting with those boys again. I told her too many times already. Don't bring that stuff into my shop. One more time and you're gone. She can't say I didn't warn her."

"She's a pip," I said.

"Tell me about it." She stared at me. "So . . . you want a job?"

"Not this one."

"I'd pay you *real* money. *Plus* donuts."

"I love your donuts too much to be around them all the time," I told her. "If I worked here, smelling them, eating them every day, they would stop being so special to me. When I walk in your door I want to be thrilled."

She looked at me as if I were daffy. She shrugged—"Okay, have it your way"—and went on sweeping.

I thought of Betty Lou. Who would bring her donuts every Monday now? I asked Margie.

"Same as always," she said. "I'd never forget Betty Lou. When I fired the kid, she said she's still gonna come for Betty Lou's donuts on Mondays. Fine, I said."

Good for you, Alvina, I thought.

"Sounds like she's not mad at you for firing her," I said.

"She's never mad at me," she said. "She knows I don't take any guff."

"So," I said, "you know Betty Lou?"

"Sure. We graduated together. She was a looker in those days. Dogwood Festival. She was in the Court."

"She told me."

"Should have been Queen."

"Really?"

"Really. Her problem was, she wasn't flashy enough. Her hair was mousy. Plain clothes. No pizzazz. Shy. Never talked. The best-looking girl in the class, but you had to strain to see it. It's a wonder she made the Court. Probably got the votes of all the other shy violets."

Margie was at the counter now, using a marker on a sheet of paper. She held it up to me. It said HELP WANTED. She found a roll of tape and fixed it to the shopwindow. She gave the front door a punch. "Doggone that girl. She was a great sweeper."

September 5

Speaking of Alvina . . .

I got a phone call today from her mother. She started off saying Alvina "always speaks well" of me and that I seem to be one of the few friends she has these days. She said she appreciated how I handled the Calamity of the Broken Fingernail, and she was very happy with my work in the garden. Which was all very nice, but I wondered what she was getting at. She asked me if I knew Alvina had been "dismissed" from her job at Margie's. I said yes, I had heard. She said did I know Alvina had been home from school today? I said no. She said, "Well, she was. She was suspended for one day." Her voice snagged on the word "suspended."

"Can you guess why?" she said.

"Fighting?" I said, maybe too quickly.

"Yes," she said. "And the school year is just beginning. I'm afraid to think what lies ahead. She seems to be getting worse."

I thought of Alvina's stare down with Dootsie across the table at Margie's. I thought of her promise to continue delivering Betty Lou's donuts even after she'd been fired. "Mrs. Klecko," I said, "I know I don't have any business saying this to you because you already knew it long before me, but Alvina is a good kid. I think there's nothing wrong that a little time won't cure. I think she's just sort of caught between dolls and boys."

There was silence on the other end of the line. I got the impression that Mrs. Klecko was composing herself. Finally she said, "Thank you. I think so too. At least I hope so. In the meantime"—she gave a little chuckle—"we've all got to live through it, don't we?"

I chuckled. "That we do."

"So . . . I have a big favor to ask of you—and I want to make it clear right up front that we would insist on paying you for this—her father and I were wondering if you would be willing to take Alvina under your wing, so to speak. For a little while. Maybe you can smooth out the rough edges. She likes you."

I didn't know what to say, so I just said, "Wow."

"Daunting?"

"Yes, I guess so. It's not how I picture myself, in charge of somebody. I don't know if I want that much responsibility for another person."

"It's not like that. You wouldn't be 'in charge of' her. We're not asking you to come up with some sort of program. We're just asking you to be around her. Hang out with her. Take her with you now and then when you go someplace."

"So you're not expecting, like, a boot camp?"

She laughed. "Oh please, no. Just be yourself, that's all. Big sister without the bossiness. Hopefully something will rub off on her."

Well, I still wasn't comfortable with the whole idea, but

I finally said okay, but only if she promised not to pay me. She agreed. So now I'm Alvina's—gulp!—big sister.

September 6

Every day so far I've been putting an orange half on top of the barbecue. Today I put it three houses down the back alley, on the roof of a toolshed.

September 7

We went to the mall today—my new "little sister" Alvina and me on our bikes, Dootsie in her cart behind me. They had the school day off, I played hooky. Dootsie wanted a Babar the Elephant lunch box. She didn't want to take her lunch to school in it. She just wanted to carry the lunch box.

She forgot about the lunch box as soon as she spotted Piercing Pagoda. "I wanna nose ring!" she cried, pulling me toward the mid-aisle stall.

"No," I told her. "You already have your ears pierced. Your mother would not allow it."

She hugged me. "You're my boss now. You can say yes." She turned up the charm. *"Pleeeeease."*

"You're wasting your adorable face," I told her. "Besides, they don't even do noses here."

She stomped her foot. "Bullpoopy."

"I want a tattoo," said Alvina. Just as I was turning to

respond, a hand flashed out and slapped the back of her head and three boys went racing by. Alvina screamed, "I'll kill you!" and started after them, but she jerked to a halt because my hand was tight on the back of her collar. "Oww!" she squawked. "You broke my *neck*."

"Sorry," I said. At that moment I was glad she wasn't my real little sister.

She reached for my hand. "Let *go*."

"No, Alvina," I said. "*You* let go. You're not a warrior. You're an eleven-year-old girl."

Dootsie poked her leg. "You're a human *bean*."

The boys were down by Auntie Anne's now. They were facing us, laughing. One of them was the blond-haired boy—the picture on her bedroom door. It was his hand that had slapped her. Back in May at the Dogwood Festival, Alvina had beaten him up. Bloodied him. Embarrassed him. *Beat up by a girl!* Another boy might have slunk home and crawled under his bed and never come out again. But here he was, still with his buddies, facing his tormentor, thumbing his nose at her. I liked this kid.

Alvina was pulling on my arm like a dog on a leash. She pointed up the mall. "Yer dead meat! Yer roadkill!"

I wrapped my arm around her and pulled her close. She was panting.

Dootsie looked up at her in fear and fascination. "You gonna beat 'em up, Alvina?"

"No," I said, "Alvina is not going to beat anybody up. Alvina is going to find out that boys are people too. They're not the enemy. Alvina is going to learn that fighting is not the only way to deal with them."

I took each girl by the hand and led them in the opposite direction from the boys. We found Dootsie's lunch box. And a DVD for Alvina. It was my treat. I told her she could pick anything she wanted as long as it was in the comedy section. She groaned and tried to steer me to horror, but finally she gave in and chose *The Nutty Professor*.

We junked it up for lunch. Chocolate-cherry cheesecake and ice cream sodas at the Cheesecake Factory. (They didn't have strawberry-banana smoothies.) The girls sat across the table from me. Dootsie kept spooning whipped cream from the top of Alvina's soda. I kept telling her to stop it. "You have plenty of your own." She ignored me, giggling with every new theft. To my surprise, Alvina did not seem especially bothered. Every time Dootsie dug her spoon into Alvina's whipped cream, Alvina simply took a spoonful of hers. And then Dootsie snatched Alvina's cherry and popped it into her mouth, and before Alvina could retaliate, Dootsie had devoured her own cherry as well. Alvina smacked her on the hand with her long-handled spoon. The giggling stopped. Dootsie's eyes got huge as she stared in disbelief at the smear of whipped cream left on her hand. Alvina was now concentrating on her soda as if nothing had happened. Dootsie's lip began to quiver.

"Dootsie, come over here with me now," I said. I pulled her soda to my side. Dootsie came over.

We ate our cheesecake and slurped our ice cream sodas

in silence for a while. Then I said, "Alvina, have you ever heard of counting coup?"

"No," she said.

"It's a tradition from Native Americans," I said. "You want to hear how it goes?"

"No."

"Okay, good. I'll tell you, then. It has to do with honor and the idea that there's more honor in touching than in killing. Say you're a member of a tribe and you're at war with another tribe. If you killed a member of the other tribe, that would be a big honor for you. If they had such a thing as trophies then, you'd probably get the biggest one."

Dootsie grumped, "I didn't get a tropy for Mrs. Blob."

I patted her hand. "Someday." I turned back to Alvina. "But there was an even greater honor, an honor that would live forever. If you wanted this greatest honor of all, you would not *kill* that other warrior. What you would do was you would sneak up on him and just *touch* him—like maybe just lay the point of your spear on his shoulder for a second— then off you go. And for the rest of your life you get to tell the story of how brave you were to get that close to your enemy and not even hurt him. And for generations to come your children and great-great-grandchildren will re- peat your story around the campfire, and you will become a legend."

Dootsie was all ears and open mouth. Alvina was noisily slurping the last of her soda, but I knew she was listening. I reached down and touched Dootsie's shoulder with my fingertip. "That," I said, "is called counting coup."

We walked the mall some more. Dootsie got tired and tugged on me. "Carry me." I lugged her around for a while, and as soon as I put her down Alvina said, "Carry me." I chuckled at her little joke, but her face was its usual stone self when she repeated, "Carry me."

I stared at her. "You're serious?"

"Okay, fine," she said. "Don't." She walked away.

I snatched at her, hoisted her up, and carried her through the mall as long as my arms held out. We got some strange looks and Dootsie got plenty jealous.

On the way home, if Dootsie stuck out her fingertip and touched Alvina's shoulder once, she did it a hundred times, each time saying, "Coo to yoo." By the end, Alvina was losing her battle not to laugh.

September 8

Do you know what day this is, Leo?

It's our anniversary. Two years.

The first time we saw each other.

Two years ago today—two turns around the sun—I walked through the lunchroom at Mica High with my ukulele, captivated by one pair of eyes staring at me, your eyes, terrified that I would sing to you. And though I passed by your table and went on to sing to someone else, I did leave something behind with you: my heart. Of course, you didn't know it at the time. Maybe I didn't either. What have you done with my heart, Leo? Have you taken good care of it? Have you misplaced it?

September 10

I think I'll do this in a kind of shorthand from now on. Make it more fun for you.

O of course will stand for Orange.

Then comes the = sign, meaning I Set One Out Again Today.

Then (A), meaning Alley behind Street Address That Follows.

Or (BY), meaning Backyard.

Then the Street Address.

Then (F) for Fence.

Or (P) for Pole.

Or (SE) for Something Else.

So, for today . . .

O = (A)219RappsDam(F)

Got that? Today I put an *Orange* on a *Fence* in the *Alley* behind *219 Rapps Dam Rd.*

Curious?

Mystified?

September 12

I was downtown buying buttons for my mother—she's making costumes for a production of *The Pirates of Penzance* at People's Light & Theater—when I saw Perry. He was coming out of Pizza Dee-Lite. He turned the other way and walked up Bridge St., so he didn't see me. We were probably the only kids on the streets this Wednesday morning: me the homeschooler, him the renegade truant.

He had a slice of pizza in one hand, a paper cup in the other. He shook the hand with the pizza and a piece of tissue paper fluttered to the sidewalk. He ate the pizza slice in about three bites. He seemed to eat half the crust, then tossed the rest into the street. He gulped his drink and tossed the cup into the gutter. I could hear him belch. All this happened within the space of one block.

I was fuming. I called: "Ever hear of a *trash can?*"

He turned. When he saw it was me, he smiled and waved. "Hey."

I walked up to him. "I said, ever hear of a trash can?"

His smile disappeared. He took a Snickers bar from his pocket, pulled the wrapper halfway down, held it out to me. "Want a bite?"

"No," I said.

He chomped off half the bar. He stood there chewing in front of me, looking at me. "How's Dootsie?" he said.

"None of your business," I said.

He laughed, spewing peanut bits.

"What's so funny?" I said.

"*I* was just going to say that."

"This may come as shocking news to you," I said, "but this happens to be the world I live in, and so maybe it *is* my business."

He put the rest of the candy bar in his mouth, crumpled up the wrapper, and tossed it over his shoulder. His eyes never wavered from mine.

"You're crapping up my world," I said.

He grinned. "You could say I'm crapping up my *own* world."

"Exactly."

His tongue came out and felt around his mouth, mopping up stray chocolate and pizza sauce.

"Exactly," he said. "So, what, no homeschool today?"

"Stop changing the subject."

"What was the subject?"

He started walking. I didn't have much choice but to go along.

"The subject is you and your habits."

"My crappy habits."

"Your crappy habits."

"They bother you."

"You could say that."

"Do you have any crappy habits?" His voice was steady and pleasant. You might have thought we were discussing *Ondine* or something.

"You're changing the subject again," I said.

He snapped his fingers. "Forgot. That's another bad habit I have, changing the subject." He put his finger in the air. "Okay . . . subject . . . crap . . . crap . . ." He put his finger to his lips, pretended to ponder. He looked directly at me. "Okay. The world is crappy already. What harm is more crap going to do? If the world's a dump, then everything is garbage." He shrugged. He smiled. "Okay?"

I just stared at him. His face tilted and came toward me. For an instant I thought he was going to kiss me, but he tapped me on the forehead. "Hello in there?"

"*If* the world's a dump," I said.

He grabbed my hand and shook it mockingly. "That's what I said. Congratulations."

"But the world isn't a dump."

"Says you."

"But you believe it is."

"Says I."

I stared at him some more. I didn't know where to start. "You're wrong."

He shrugged. "Sue me."

"You can't believe—"

"I can believe anything I want."

He continued walking. I followed. I was beginning to realize how little I knew about him.

"Why?" I said.

He laughed. "We're back where we started." He put on a petulant little-kid voice: "Nunna your business."

"So what am I supposed to do?" I said. "Cheer you on—'Yay, Perry!'—when you steal and junk up the town?"

He wagged his finger in my face. "You're not *supposed* to do anything. *You're* the one trying to change *me*. Remember? As far as *I'm* concerned, *you* can do anything you want."

"Except criticize you."

"Hey," he said, "if that's how you want to spend your life, getting on my case"—he threw out his arms—"be my guest." He turned his deep blue eyes on me. "And anyway—" He let it hang there. He was smirking.

Suddenly I felt as if I were on roller skates. "What?"

"I know why you're doing it."

I stopped. He walked on.

"Doing what?" I said. "What? Why?" I think I was babbling.

He flipped his answer as blithely as a candy wrapper over his shoulder: "You know."

September 14

Morning Lenape ad:

> **He says the world is a bad place**
> **but I've seen him on the high dive,**
> **the pride in his eyes.**

September 15

Dori Dilson wrote and told me where you're going to college. I like knowing where you are. I will always know where you are.

September 16

$O = (BY)303RappsDam(P)$

September 22

It's not a Thursday but I went to Calendar Hill anyway, because today is the Autumnal Equinox. Autumn begins. On this day the sun at noon is directly above the equator, meaning that day and night are equal. From now on until Winter Solstice, night will be longer than day. The light is leaving.

I had to pedal hard to get to the hill in time to plant today's marker. I barely made it before the sun. I'm still getting used to living without clocks and watches. The main thing is getting myself up in time on Calendar days. When I go to bed the night before, I say to myself: *When the sun is a bike ride away, I will hear it. It will sound like wind in treetops. I will awaken.* And it works!

My father wasn't too happy that day when he came home to a house without clocks. "How's a milkman supposed to wake up at two a.m. without an alarm clock?" he said.

We had to admit it was a good question.

"Well, then I guess you'll just have to sleep in the basement," my mother said, sending me a wink. "Alarms at two a.m. are no longer part of my life."

So my father bought himself a wristwatch with a tiny alarm that peeps him awake in the morning but lets my mother sleep. He couldn't bear to see us take the hammer to his old watch, so he left it on a park bench for someone to find. Actually, he's been pretty cool with the whole thing. After all, within the last year he moved from Arizona to Pennsylvania and from electronics engineer to milkman, so this was no big deal. My dad is very flexible.

All these little glitches aside, I have to tell you I *love* living in a world without clocks. The shackles are gone. I'm a puppy unleashed in a meadow of time. As I watched the sun come up this morning, I felt a new sense of kinship with it. Something primitive stirred inside me, something that remembers the rising sun by itself, before there were minutes and schedules and calendars, before there were even words like "morning."

Days till Solstice: 90

September 28

I took my new sister, Alvina, on a milk run today. Her mother loved the idea. She was waiting with Alvina on the front step. She waved as her daughter climbed into the truck. "Have fun!" she called.

I had forgotten that seating would be a problem, since the jump seat my father had installed for me was the only provision for passengers. Alvina and I scrunched onto the seat. "I don't believe you're doing this to me," she grumped. "It's still dark." I grinned and nodded at my father. I had told him not to expect the cheeriest kid in the world. And then Alvina got up and without a word plopped herself down on my lap. Within seconds she was sleeping, her head lolling back against my shoulder.

She didn't have long to doze, as my father soon pulled the truck up to Ridgeview Diner. "Breakfast time," I said. I half led, half dragged her into the diner.

We took a booth at the windows. Alvina slumped in her seat, grumbled, "I don't believe this," and went immediately back to sleep.

"You still sure this is a great idea?" my father said.

When the waitress came and said, "Coffee, folks?" I shook Alvina awake. The waitress must have been wondering why we had this child out in the middle of the night.

"Alvina," I said, "what do you want to drink? Milk? Tea?"

Her chin was on her chest, her eyes closed. "Coffee."

"No coffee," I said. "You're a kid."

"Always have coffee," she mumbled. "Want coffee."

I knew she was lying. I knew that eleven-year-olds and

caffeine were not a great mix. But this whole day would be wasted if she slept through it. I looked at my father. He nodded.

"Okay," I said to the waitress. "Three coffees."

Ten minutes later Alvina was awake and the waitress was setting a stack of pancakes and bacon in front of her. The waitress tapped Alvina's fingernail. "Snazzy."

Alvina sliced at her pancakes and made her who-let-you-in face. "*Snazzy?*"

The waitress fluttered her own fingernails over the table. "Check out mine." Hers were deep red with pink squiggles.

Alvina made a huffy show of patience and took a look. "Mine is better," she said, and returned to her slicing.

The waitress frowned, studied her nails, nodded, said, "You're right," gave me a quick grin, and breezed off. "Enjoy your breakfast."

My father started in on his grilled sticky bun. He pointed his fork at the fingernail. "Very impressive. I'll bet it brings the boys running."

"I hate boys," said Alvina. She started pouring syrup over her pancakes.

"Boys are rats," said my father.

"Hey," I said, "I happen to be the mother of a rat."

"Sorry, forgot. Boys are weasels."

The syrup bottle was half empty and still she poured. I took it away from her.

I knew my father was trying to get a rise out of Alvina, but it wasn't coming. Still, he plowed on: "At the age of ten, every boy in the world should be turned upside down and a worm should be dropped into each nostril."

I cracked up. I spewed half-chewed sticky bun all over my plate. Alvina just went on eating, didn't raise an eyebrow.

I could feel my father percolating. He wasn't going down without a fight. My dad has a peculiar kind of radar that senses resistance to smiling. If there's a grump anywhere between himself and the horizon, he seems to know it. Not only that, he feels he has to do something about it. I think of it as a harmless obsessive-compulsive disorder. Also, there was the clam-up factor. Most kids—so I've heard—clam up in front of adults. But my father has been spoiled—he's had me chattering in his ear for sixteen years. And now Dootsie. He's not used to an untalkative kid.

"There's a theory," he said, aiming himself at Alvina, who was aiming herself at the pancakes, "that boys are actually a different species from girls. Some scientists believe boys are descended from small, smelly mammals. Possibly skunks."

He waited for a response. None came. Alvina poured syrup on her bacon.

"So, Alvina . . . ," he said, "what do *you* think?"

"About what?" she said, mush-mouthed.

"About what I just said."

"Whud you say?"

My father's eyes rolled up. I think it was dawning on him that this could be his greatest challenge yet.

Silently I mouthed to him: *I warned you.*

"So, Alvina . . . ," he said, "cool necklace."

She didn't respond. As usual, Pooh Bear's smiling face contrasted with hers.

"Do you have one cool toenail too?"

"No."

I knew what he was doing. He was tapping around her shell, probing for a soft spot.

"So, Alvina . . . you hate boys. Does that mean you hate them all?"

"Yeah."

"Every single one in the world?"

"Yeah."

"Including me? I'm a boy."

"You're a milkman."

"I hear you have a brother. How about him? He's a boy."

"Him especially."

My father whistled softly. "You're a tough cookie." He aimed his fork at her pancakes. "Can I have a little piece?"

"No."

He made a pouty lip. "Just one teeny piece?"

Alvina looked up from her plate and glared directly into his eyes. She enunciated fiercely: *"No."*

The fork withdrew. This was more entertaining than *The Blob.*

My father sent me a glance and a grin and started in again. "So, Alvina . . . I know you hate all boys, but I'll bet there's one special boy. One that you hate more than all the others combined—right?"

Alvina just munched for a while. Then she shrugged. "Maybe."

"Does he go to school with you?"

"Maybe."

"Do you think about him sometimes? I mean, how much you hate him? You think about how you'd like to torture him? Like, dumping a whole wheelbarrowful of stinging ants on him? Stuff like that?"

She shrugged. "Maybe."

"Yeah," he said, "I know what you mean. I hated somebody like that once."

She popped the last piece of pancake into her mouth. "Yeah?"

"Yeah. We were in seventh grade. She was in my homeroom. I hated her more than anybody in the world."

"Yeah?"

"Yeah. Know what I did to her?"

She was all eyes and ears. "What?"

He grinned. He pointed to his ring finger. "I married her."

I wanted to stand and applaud, but I restrained myself. Alvina just rolled her eyes and wrinkled her nose as if a bad smell had come through the door.

My eyes accidentally landed on the clock above the pie case. "Dad, we're already late."

But my father was on a roll. Like me, he doesn't know when enough is enough.

"So, Alvina . . . how old are you?"

She poured syrup into the cold remainder of her coffee. We hadn't allowed her a refill.

"Eleven and three-quarters."

"You sure it's not eleven and four-fifths?"

She shrugged. "Could be."

"Well," he said with exaggerated dismay, "that's too bad."

She took a sip of the cold, syrupy coffee, decided she liked it, and gulped down the rest. Then looked up at him, debating whether to ask the obvious question. She did. "Why's that?"

He wagged his head grimly. If you hadn't known my father, you'd have thought he had just come from a funeral. "Why? Because you're coming to the end of a beautiful, wonderful time. Your kidhood is almost over. You know what happens next, don't you?"

Experience had taught Alvina nothing—she rose to the bait again. "What?"

"Twelve. That's what happens. And you know what then?"

She didn't really want to answer such a dumb question, but she couldn't resist finding out where all this nonsense was leading. "Thirteen," she said.

My father snapped her a finger-point. "Exactly! In other

words, you'll become a teenager." He sighed mournfully. "Such a shame."

Alvina looked at me, at him. "Why?"

"Why? Because you know what they say."

"Who's they?"

I thought: *Score one for you, girl.*

My father ignored the question. "They say teenagers are rotten. They go from being cute and cuddly little kids to monsters who want to stay out late and walk a block behind their parents."

I was a little uneasy. I knew my father was just toying with her, trying to provoke her, but I wasn't sure if Alvina knew. She took a long look at me. I think, for once, she *saw* me. She seemed about to say something, and I swear I could see the words forming on the other side of her lips: *Stargirl isn't rotten.* But they never came out. She twiddled her spoon in the empty coffee cup. She shook her head. "Not me."

My father and I were both caught by surprise. The spoon twiddled in the cup. Finally my father prompted her. "Not you?"

The twiddling stopped. She stared into the cup. "No. I'm backwards. I'm a rotten kid now, but I'll be an amazing teenager."

I know it didn't really happen this way, but the whole diner seemed to catch its breath, as if sensing that something remarkable had just been uttered and that it must be properly framed in silence. My father and I looked at each other. I fought off tears. Alvina resumed her twiddling.

At last my father reached across the table and placed his hand over hers. "I think you're right, Alvina. Except for one thing."

She didn't look up. She didn't need to say, *What?*

"You are *not* a rotten kid."

She turned away. She gazed out the window into the night.

We were on our way then. I explained Alvina's job to her: she would fetch the order notes and used bottles from the customers' front steps, she would read the notes to me, I would fill the carrier, and my dad would deliver it. At the first house, the Turners', she reached for the carrier I had just filled and said, "Let me take it." My father didn't hesitate: "Go ahead." And off she rattled with the order for the Turners' front-step box. From then on, as long as the delivery was outside, Alvina did it.

We were running late, and the sky was graying in the east when we pulled up to 214 White Horse Road—the Huffelmeyers. 1 qt buttermk, 1 qt choc. I told Alvina to be very quiet, we were going inside. As my father turned on the fringed table lamp, she surprised me for the second time this morning—she took off her shoes. At first she stayed behind me as I pointed out my favorites in the gallery of family photos in the living and dining rooms. Then she was off by herself, moving around the rooms from picture to picture.

When my father returned from the kitchen and tapped her on the shoulder, she ignored him. "Dad," I whispered, "wait." She was utterly lost in the generations of Huffelmeyers. Several times she reached out a fingertip and touched a photo. We must have waited a good ten minutes (by clock time) before I finally grabbed her sneakers and dragged her out.

The sun rose. I thought daylight would inhibit Alvina, but it didn't. She continued to sit on my lap. And she seemed proud to have people see her working as a milk kid.

We ate lunch (breakfast for people on ordinary time) at the Creamery, where my father resumed his boy-bashing efforts to make her smile:

"When a baby boy is born, the doctor slaps its face instead of its hiney."

"What's the difference between turtles and boys? Turtles have brains."

"If you subtract all the boys from the world, you'd get an A in math."

My father kept it up for the rest of the run after lunch. To his growing frustration and her own credit, Alvina never cracked.

When we returned her to her house in mid-afternoon, she climbed down from my lap for the last time. She started off, then leaned back in and whispered in my ear: "Is your dad cuckoo or what?"

September 29

O = (BY)1334Cranberry(F)

October 5

This morning I meditated at the picnic table in the park where Dootsie came into my life. It took me longer than usual to get started, because I couldn't stop thinking of Alvina's words: *I'm a rotten kid.* Of course, I loved the words that followed, and I hoped she truly meant them; but for now, to define herself as rotten for the next year or so, well, I just wished it didn't have to be. But eventually, twitter by twit, I began to vanish. Here, now, Alvina, Stargirl—all evaporated like fizz bubbles from soda foam.

I was out of my self. I was nowhere. And everywhere. No *When.* No *Then.* Only *Now.* Existence in such a state is so pure that memory cannot get a foothold. The more successful I am in a meditation, the less I remember of it. And I remember nothing at all of my meditation today—only my entrance into it, as my last thoughts of Alvina dissolved away, and my exit out of it, when I opened my eyes to discover . . .

. . . Perry! . . .

. . . sitting next to me.

He was sitting cross-legged, his hands, palms up, cupped in his lap, back erect, shoulders square, eyes closed. Just like me. Was he mocking me? Or had he been doing this for years?

I stared at him, waiting. Not a flutter from his eyelashes. I thought of you and me in the desert, when I gave you your meditation lesson. I felt a sudden pang for you. It was all so new to you (how much of me was new to you!). You didn't understand it, you weren't very good at it—but you tried, you did your best. For me, I think.

When Perry finally opened his eyes, he continued to look straight ahead, as if I weren't there.

I said, "You lied."

Only his eyes shifted my way. "Huh?"

"You lied. You said on the roof you don't meditate."

"You're right. I lied."

"Don't you *ever* go to school?"

"Don't *you?*"

"I *am* in school," I said. "This is part of my homeschool."

"Advanced Meditation?"

"Elements of Nothingness. I don't think I'll ever be as good as I want." I was wondering if he was ever going to turn and really look at me. "Are you mocking me?"

He turned. "No."

"You do this a lot?"

"No."

"Are you good at it?"

"Yes. Very."

I believed him. "So this is how you escape that crappy world you live in?"

He shrugged. "I guess."

"And the roof."

"And the roof."

I looked around. "Well, congratulations. You've been here for a while and you still haven't trashed up the place."

He stuck a finger in the air. "That reminds me." He took a pack of chewing gum from his pocket. He pulled out a stick and offered it to me. I said no thanks. He unwrapped it and put it in his mouth. He crumpled the wrapper. He looked around. He grinned. He held it out to me. I took it and put it in my pocket.

"Seriously," I said, "don't you get in trouble not going to school?"

"I go," he said. "I just get sick a lot. I'm sickly."

"Or are you just sneaking off from your harem—*Dandy?*"

"Guy's gotta have a break."

"So how's it work, Dandy? Do you go out with them one at a time? Or all at once?"

He wagged his finger. "That's classified. Secrets of the harem."

"Is the number classified too? How many Honeybees are there? Just the three I met at Pizza Dee-Lite?"

"That's all," he said. "But there's no limit. There's a slot open for number four. Want to apply?"

"Sorry," I said. "I'm not a harem kind of girl."

"You get to wear a Honeybee tattoo."

I swooned. "Where do I sign up?"

He laughed. "So you're a one-guy kind of girl, huh?"

I'm not good at playing coy, but I was trying. "Maybe."

"Arizona Leo?"

He remembered. Did that mean something?

"You have a good memory."

"The guy who dumped you."

"I never said that."

"Dootsie did."

"Dootsie lies. She admits it."

He looked off across the park. "Well, anyway, dumped or not, he's there. . . ."

"And you're here."

He threw out his arms. "Up close and personal."

I had a premonition of those arms closing around me. And a memory of yours. "Such wonders I must be missing," I said with mock dismay. "Me and my silly anti-harem principles."

He turned those deep blues on me. "Yeah. Too bad."

The words fit our quippy, flirty script, but his eyes said something else. We were still sitting cross-legged on the picnic table. Our knees were touching. I felt the need to keep chattering.

"So, is that what this is, a recruiting trip? You're trying to sign me up?"

He put on a face of mock innocence. "Where'd you get that idea? Why would I want to do that?"

"That was answered back at Pizza Dee-Lite—you think I'm fascinating."

"Stephanie said that. I said 'interesting.'"

"So"—I nudged his knee—"what is it you find so *fascinating* about me?"

"Interesting."

"I prefer *fascinating*."

He pretended to think. "Well . . . for one thing, you're not a typical girl."

"Old news. I already told you that on the roof that night."

"You were right."

"And you were wrong."

He sighed. "Mea culpa."

"So," I said, "*how* am I not typical?"

"You want specifics?"

"I want specifics. I want details. I want flattery."

He turned himself ninety degrees so he was now facing me broadside. His stare was a blue-eyed laser that seemed to peel the skin from me.

"You have freckles across your nose. They spill onto your cheeks a little."

"Piddlefoo. Freckles are common."

"Eleven."

I boggled. "You *counted* them?" I had never counted them myself.

"In the library that day. While you were yelling at me."

"You were spitting lemon seeds all over the library. And I did not yell. I berated. What else?"

He stared some more. I was uncomfortable being a target in profile, so I rotated a quarter turn. Now we were face to face, knees to knees.

"You don't wear designer labels."

"I hate labels." I looked him over. "I guess you hate them too."

He seemed to wince at that, then said simply, "Yeah."

I regretted my words as soon as I said them. The shirt he was wearing was the same one he wore every time I saw him. He lived in a little space behind a bike and lawn mower repair shop. He stole food. He shopped in Dumpsters. Hate had nothing to do with Perry Delloplane and labels. He was simply poor.

It was in me to apologize, but he would say, "Why?" and I would have to reply, and I was afraid to bring the subject out into the open. So I tried to steer us back to safer ground. "So that's it? Labels and freckles?"

"You're not stuck on yourself. You don't touch your hair every ten seconds. You don't look into a mirror every five minutes. You don't wear makeup."

"I plucked my eyebrows once."

"Not lately."

We laughed.

"You don't act like you're gorgeous."

"Even though I am, right?"

"No, you're not." He said it so casually, I knew he meant it. "Neither are most girls. But that doesn't stop them from acting like it."

"Wait a minute. Let's go back to the part where I'm *not* gorgeous."

His eyebrows arched innocently. "Problem?"

He had me feeling wobbly again. Talking with this guy never seems to go the way I want.

I shrugged. "Well, I guess not. Not if beauty is in the eye of the beholder—and you're the only beholder I see around here."

He nodded. "Good."

"So," I said, "let me get this straight. I'm typical because I'm *not* gorgeous, and I'm *not* typical because I don't act as if I *am* gorgeous."

"Something like that."

"So . . . if I'm not gorgeous, what am I?"

He grinned. "You're asking for a label?"

I grinned. "Touché."

He made a bubble with his chewing gum and popped it. "So what's his last name?"

I flinched. "What? Who? Where'd *that* come from?"

"Arizona Leo. The guy who didn't dump you."

"I'm not finished with the other conversation yet. I want to know more reasons why you like me."

He held up a warning finger. "Hey, I said you're interesting—"

"Fascinating."

"—fascinating. I never said I like you."

I did a mopping-the-brow pantomime. "Oh good. That's a relief. Because I don't like you either. Wouldn't that have been icky if we didn't agree?"

He spat out his chewing gum. "Icky."

"Borlock."

He nodded, smiling. "Leo Borlock." He pulled out another stick of gum. He handed me the wrapper. "Leo Borlock, huh?" He seemed to chew on both the gum and the name. I felt a flurry of questions about you coming on, but instead he said, "Oh yeah, the calendar."

"Huh?"

A conversation with Perry Delloplane is about as straightforward as the path of a soccer ball.

"Your calendar. That's pretty not typical too."

"Really?" I said. "You don't think many girls plant a spatula in a farmer's field every week and at the end of the year wind up with a big homemade sundial to celebrate the Winter Solstice? You don't think so?"

"Not girls *or* boys."

"So you're impressed."

"Sort of."

"Just sort of?"

"Very sort of."

"And your crappy home planet, does it have a Solstice? Does the sun ever rise on Poop World?"

His reply wasn't the grin and quip I expected, just: "Once in a while."

"Well then"—I paused, plunged—"do I have a treat for you. How would you like to join this impressive, fascinating girl next time she goes to plant a sunrise marker on Calendar Hill?"

He didn't hesitate. "Sure."

I remembered waiting for him on that morning back in

August, hoping. I reminded myself that I had not specifically invited him that time. I wouldn't make the same mistake now.

I tapped his knee. "Thursday morning. This is Friday. That's six days from now. Can you remember?"

"I can count to six."

"*Before* sunrise."

"Before sunrise."

I told him where it is. I had never seen him on a bicycle. "Can you get there?"

"Yeah."

"Can you wake up early enough?" I knew I was pushing too hard, but I couldn't help myself. "You have an alarm clock?"

"I don't need alarm clocks."

"Me neither," I said. "I live in a house without clocks."

"Me too."

I believed it. I think he would be a clockless person, rich or poor. We seemed to intersect at many points. Suddenly I felt flirty again. "So, jealous?"

This time he was the one taken off guard. "Huh?"

"Of Leo?"

He grinned. "No comment."

"You know," I said with an air, "Leo said the same thing to me once, the first time I ever had a real conversation with him."

"Really?"

"Really. He was already starstruck—so to speak. I had

sent him a valentine card and tweaked his ear in the lunch-room and, you know, just generally overwhelmed him with my charms. I think you can relate to that."

"Right."

"Right. But he was so shy and absolutely terrified of me. So he still had not spoken a single word to me. And then this one night I looked out the window and I saw him walking up and down the street in front of my house, trying to work up the nerve to make a move."

"Did he?" Perry's expression and voice said, *I'm really not interested,* but I knew that was a mask.

"No. So I did. As soon as I opened the front door he ducked behind our car in the driveway. We talked, but we never laid eyes on each other. At least not directly. Cinnamon scooted under the car and went to him. So at least Cinnamon saw him. I asked him if he thought I was cute."

"Wha'd he say?"

"That's a silly question. A resounding *Yes!* of course. And that's when I asked him if he thought Cinnamon was cute too, and that's when he said, 'No comment.'"

"You remember everything people say to you?"

I locked into his eyes. "Everything *some* people say to me."

We fell silent. We just looked at each other, sitting cross-legged on the picnic table. As in my meditations, I had no awareness of time passing, only a sense of the air between us electrified with eyes.

When we got down from the table, I found, to my

surprise, that I was chewing gum. We walked off through the park, and I think we were both relieved to turn our talk to safer subjects, idle chitchat, anything but ourselves.

October 6

I know you have questions, Leo. And I know you're busy with other things at college. So I'll ask them for you:

YOU: Do you like him?

ME: Yes.

YOU: Love him?

ME: Next question.

YOU: I hear he counted your freckles.

ME: He did! You believe it?

YOU: He likes you, doesn't he?

ME: Mm . . . yes.

YOU: Yes, but?

ME: He's a rolling stone. His nickname is Dandy. He has a harem.

YOU: And you want him all to yourself.

ME: I didn't say that.

YOU: Maybe you're afraid if you get too close to him he'll dump you.

ME: Maybe.

YOU: Like I did.

ME: I wish you wouldn't put it that way.

YOU: But I did. I dumped you. And I'm sorry. I regret it now.

ME: Hey—enough! This is *my* fantasy interview. I'll give you your lines.

YOU: Sorry.

ME: Speaking of sorry, why don't you ask me if I feel sorry for him.

YOU: Do you feel sorry for him?

ME: "Sorry" doesn't sound right. Maybe "caring."

YOU: Would you like to fix his crappy world?

ME: I can't fix his world. Maybe I can fix him. A little bit, at least.

YOU: How?

ME: Oh, I don't know. Maybe just by being around him. He handed me his chewing gum wrappers yesterday. That's a start.

YOU: Fixing a person—some people might call you a busybody.

ME: So be it.

YOU: So, with this Perry guy here, what are we talking about—a reclamation project or a budding romance?

ME: I'll let you decide.

YOU: Are you surprised he hasn't tried to kiss you yet?

ME: Yes.

YOU: Do you want him to?

ME: Yes.

YOU: What about me?

ME: No comment.

October 7

O = (BY)210Birch(F)

October 8

I met Alvina after school. I did the most basic kid thing you can do: I took her to Pizza Dee-Lite. I prayed her enemy boys wouldn't show up. They didn't. She threw a small fit because a mushroom from my half of the pizza wound up on her pepperoni half. Otherwise she was harmlessly unpleasant. As per Mrs. Klecko's instructions, I simply tried to be myself. I have a feeling I'm not rubbing off on her.

October 9

Margie has a new helper. A woman. She does what Alvina did—sweeps, helps out in the kitchen, keeps the coffee going. Except she gets paid in real money, not donuts. Her name is Neva. Margie introduced her to me, saying I'm her "best customer." "Hi," I said. "Neat name." "Thanks," she said, and went back to the coffee urn. Not exactly chummy. Suddenly grumpy Alvina wasn't looking so bad.

Neva looks to be maybe in her late thirties, forty. Her brown hair is long and curly and streaked with blond highlights. She wears dangling earrings and oodles of makeup. You might say she's glamorous (from the neck up), but you hardly notice because she's so shy. She doesn't speak.

She doesn't look at Margie when Margie speaks to her. She doesn't look up when the door tinkles and someone comes in. She wears a huge, gaudy diamond that must be a fake. She wears loose dresses. I guess she has to, because she's pregnant. Very.

October 10

Tomorrow is Thursday. Calendar Hill day.

October 11

He wasn't there. I can't believe it.

This time I didn't hang around waiting for him. I planted the marker and ran back to the house. I told my mother I felt like taking a ride. I pedaled to Betty Lou's house. The sun was just now coming up. I knew she was still sleeping but I didn't care. I punched the bell until she opened the door. She was so shocked when she saw me that she took a step outside the doorway. When she realized where she was, she shuddered, pulled me inside, and slammed the door.

"Stargirl, what's the matter?"

I started to tell her.

"Wait—" she said. She led me by the hand into the kitchen. She made coffee and put out donuts. She took a seat at the opposite end of the table. Then she grabbed another chair and pulled it close to me. She took my hand. She rubbed it. She studied my face. "I've never seen you this

angry. Come to think of it, I've never seen you angry at all."
She studied me some more. She cupped her hands over my
ears, pulled them away, put them back, pulled them away.
"I'm making smoke signals from the steam coming out of
your ears."

A chuckleball escaped before I could stop it. "Don't
make me laugh, Betty Lou. I'm not in the mood."

She dropped the smile. "I know. Sometimes I make
light of things at the wrong time. I guess I think anyone
lucky enough to have a mockingbird outside her window
can never have a bad day." She petted my hand. "So . . .
tell."

I told her about the day at the picnic table and Perry's
no-show today. "I'm so mad I almost didn't stop here. I almost rode all the way to his house."

"So you're feeling jilted. Do you know that word? It's
old-fashioned."

I nodded. "I know it. Yes. I feel jilted."

"Because he said he would meet you and he didn't."

"Yes."

"And you can't believe it because the other day the
sparks were really flying, so to speak."

"Yes."

She pushed the donuts in front of me. I shook my head.
"Not hungry."

She sighed—"Love trumps appetite"—chose one for herself, and took a bite.

"It's not love," I said. "I mean, I don't know *what* it is."

She chewed, thinking. She stared into my eyes with soft intensity. "It's more than anger, isn't it?"

I blinked. "Is it?"

"You're confused."

"Yes."

"Befuddled."

"Yes."

"One of my all-time favorite words—'befuddled.' It sounds exactly like what it is, doesn't it?" She stood and threw up her arms and gazed at the ceiling with as pure a look of befuddlement as I've ever seen. She cried out: "Befuddled!"

I wagged my head, giggling in spite of myself. "Good grief, Betty Lou. I get the point."

She sat back down, muttering, "Befuddled . . . befuddled . . ." under her breath. It occurred to me that Betty Lou sometimes became theatrical because, confined to her house, she was her own best entertainment.

She became serious again. "Of course you're befuddled. How could you not be? He seeks you out and he sneaks up beside you during your meditation—which, by the way, was a *very* impressive thing to do—and sends you all kinds of romantic signals—and then he breaks his promise and doesn't show up for your date on Calendar Hill."

"That seems to be the way he is," I said. "He even has a reputation for it. His harem girls call him a rolling stone."

She nodded. "Well, you know what they say—a rolling stone gathers no permanent girlfriends."

"I'm not asking for permanence," I said.

This time her stare was intense without the softness. "What *are* you asking for, Galaxy Girl?"

Good question.

"I don't know. Something. *Something.* Instead of nothing."

"Well now"—she wagged her finger at me—"aren't you being a little unfair to him? It's not nothing. It's Perry—what's his last name?"

"Delloplane."

"It's Perry Delloplane—and whatever comes with him. It is what it is. Maybe you're trying too hard to put a name on it."

"Labels," I said.

She nodded. "Exactly."

"I told him I hate labels. Maybe I was kidding myself."

"Or maybe you're merely uncomfortable with uncertainty. Like the rest of the human race."

"So at least I have company."

She laughed. "Lots of it. And that means you're sitting in a classroom of billions, trying to learn the same lesson as the rest of us."

"Which is?"

"Which is: How to Be Comfortable with Uncertainty."

I waited for more. All she said was, "Warm your coffee?"

"No," I said. "So, are you going to tell me how? Give me a hint?"

Her eyes went wide. Her fingers fluttered on her breast. "As Miss Piggy would say: *moi?* I'm astounded that you think that I, a mere small-town agoraphobic, would have the answer to one of life's great questions." She bowed her head over the donuts. "I am flattered."

"Good," I said. "Now if you can put the flattery behind you, I'd appreciate an answer."

She struck a pose of sagely ponder. "Well then . . . I do believe that if anyone has the key, it may be the Buddhists."

"The Buddhists."

"Yes, the Buddhists. You know what they say—well, of course they say many things. You would do well to read the Buddhists. They come out of the East, but they have much to say to us westerners of the modern age. I remember one day when I was about twenty-eight—"

"Betty Lou"—I pressed my finger to her lips—"answer, please."

"Ah, yes, the answer. Live today. There."

"Live today."

"Yes. Live today. Not yesterday. Not tomorrow. Just today. Inhabit your moments. Don't rent them out to tomorrow. Do you know what you're doing when you spend a moment wondering how things are going to turn out with Perry?"

"What am I doing?"

"You're cheating yourself out of today. Today is calling to you, trying to get your attention, but you're stuck on tomorrow, and today trickles away like water down a drain. You wake up the next morning and that today that you wasted is gone forever. It's now yesterday. Some of those moments may have had wonderful things in store for you, but now you'll never know." She looked at me. She laughed. "Such a solemn-faced listener you are. If I were a teacher, I'd like to have thirty of you in my class."

I fumbled for my voice. "You're just . . . so right. I think when I meditate I'm trying to do that, live in the moment, but the rest of the time I think I've been pretty much a flop. Lately, anyway."

She laughed again. "Welcome to Floptown. We're all flops. None of us gets it right all the time." She threw out her arms. "C'est la vie!"

I nodded. Stared at her. Looked around the room. Looked out the window. Heard the faint hush of today passing by. "Be comfortable with uncertainty, huh?"

"Embrace the mystery."

"I usually love mysteries. When I'm not in them."

"Let's hear it for mystery!"

We clinked our coffee cups and gave three cheers to mystery.

"So," she said, "still mad?"

I checked myself. I started laughing.

"What?" she said.

"Yes. I'm sorry"—I couldn't stop laughing—"but I'm still a little mad. After all that wisdom you just poured into me." Suddenly I no longer felt like laughing. "What's wrong with me?"

Her face was all softness and sympathy now. She was seeing something in me that I myself didn't want to look at. "At the risk of sounding like a know-it-all, I think I have the answer to that."

I felt my lip quiver. "Yes?"

She took my hands in hers. She spoke barely above a whisper. "You're lonely. And that's made you vulnerable. You're not at full strength."

I nodded, my eyes filling up. We just sat silently for a time, holding hands, holding more than hands.

At last she said, "And actually, I'm a little bit glad you're still mad." She handed me a Kleenex.

I sniffed. "Really?"

"I'd rather you be mad than devastated."

"You think so?"

"Oh yes. Devastation can lead to bad places."

"Such as?"

"Such as . . . groveling."

"I don't grovel."

"If you had ridden your bicycle all the way to his house this morning, what would you have done?"

"I don't know."

"You wouldn't have groveled?"

"No."

"You wouldn't have thrown yourself at him?"

"No."

"Don't ever throw yourself at a man."

"I won't."

She studied me. She nodded. "I believe you." She held out the plate of donuts. This time I took one.

I reached out and touched her. "You never jilt me, Betty Lou. I always know where I can find you."

She wagged her head with a wounded smile. "Sad but true." The smile healed. "But don't get overconfident, young lady. I may jilt you yet. My fantasy is that someday you will come to my house and ring the bell and ring the bell and I'll never open the door . . . because"—she smacked the tabletop—"I won't be here!"

October 12

YOU: You heard her.

ME: Yes.

YOU: She said you miss me.

ME: She also said live today.

YOU: Right.

ME: And you're yesterday.

YOU: Oops. But—hey—*I* never jilted you.

ME: You did worse. You turned your back on me.

YOU: Double oops.

ME: I'm just saying that for the record. I've forgiven you.

YOU: Whew! So, do you believe everything she said?

ME: Oh yes. But . . .

YOU: But?

ME: But there is one thing I didn't say to Betty Lou. One word.

YOU: What's that?

ME: Kiss.

YOU: I think I'm sorry I asked.

ME: The more he doesn't kiss me, the more I want him to.

YOU: I am. I'm officially sorry I asked.

ME: But even that's not cut-and-dried.

YOU: No?

ME: I mean, I kind of want him to and don't want him to at the same time. Does that make sense?

YOU: For anybody but you, no.

ME: I want him to, but I'm afraid.

YOU: Of what?

ME: I'm afraid I won't be befuddled anymore. I'm afraid a kiss will answer a question I'm not sure I want answered.

YOU: Which is?

ME: I think you know.

October 13

$O = (BY)340Birch(F)$

October 16

Red slipper sock in the window.

With our mothers' blessings, Dootsie and I both played hooky to help Betty Lou past her bad day. She was in fine shape by lunchtime, but we were having so much fun we stayed till after dinner.

October 18

I took Cinnamon with me to Calendar Hill today. He rode in my pocket. I think I'll take him with me every Thursday morning. At least I know how *he* feels about me.

As I walked down Rapps Dam Road I was vaguely aware of something trying to get my attention, but my head was flying off elsewhere. Then, when I reached Route 113, before crossing, I heard the barest breath of a whisper say, *Turn around.* I looked in my pocket. Cinnamon was sleeping. Then again: *Turn around.* I turned around—and there it was. As I looked back up the road all the way to my house, every porch light along the way was lit. Subconsciously I must have known it, because my flashlight was not switched on. Starting with the Cantellos, neighbor after neighbor must have passed the word along over the weeks of Thursdays until, now, my whole path was aglow. I was so touched. I stood there at the intersection of Rapps Dam Road and Route 113 and called aloud down the corridor of porch lights: "Thank you!"

October 20

"I'm gonna be a waffle!"

That's what I woke up to. I was out late last night at a play in the city with my parents. Even homeschoolers have Saturdays off, so I was sleeping in this morning. Or trying to.

Because Dootsie was straddling my back like a jockey and shaking my shoulders and bellowing: "I'm gonna be a waffle! Your mommy's gonna make me a costume for Halloween!"

I tried to growl. I tried to be as unpleasant as possible. "Dootsie, go away."

She crawled under the covers with me. She snuggled into me and whispered into my ear: "I'm gonna be a waffle."

She grabbed my head in both hands and turned my face to her. She propped open one eye with her fingers. "I'm gonna be a waffle."

I gave up. I blobbed out of bed. I put on my robe. I slunk downstairs. I drooped at the kitchen table while my mother laughed and told me how Dootsie came barging in this morning (don't tell any robbers, but my mother unlocks the front door when she gets up to make way for Dootsie's frequent early-morning visits), telling my mother she wants to be a waffle for Halloween and will she please make her a waffle costume.

My mother suggested that she could do me up as a fork. I could pretend to be eating the little waffle. "Yes! Yes! Yes! Pleeeeeeze!" Dootsie begged, but I think I'll probably pass on that and settle for taking the waffle around from house to house.

In my groggy state this morning I wouldn't have wanted to admit it, but I'm actually grateful for Dootsie's attention these days, even when it's pesty. It helps distract me from thinking about you-know-who. I've only seen him once since the no-show at Calendar Hill. It was a few days later. I was in Margie's when I saw him heading my way with two of his Honeybees. I jumped up. "I'll be back," I told Neva, the new helper, so she wouldn't clean off my table. As I ducked into the kitchen, I said to Margie, "I'm not here."

I heard the doorbell tinkle. I heard a yip or two from the girls, but that was all. My anger was no longer flaming. It had hardened to a scab over my wound. It was protecting me from being hurt again, and I wasn't about to let him rip it away, not even with an apology. Before long the doorbell tinkled again. When I stuck my head out, they were gone.

October 21

I thought I should do something with Alvina. Nothing spectacular. Just a simple walk through the park, let the gorgeous autumn colors make their pitch to her, maybe soften her ever-bristling prickles. I was about to call her when the phone rang. It was her. She didn't say hello. She just started screaming:

"I know what you're doing! You rat! You fake! I hate you!"

I blubbered out a *"Huh?"*

She told me she overheard her parents talking about my assignment, about taking her under my wing. I tried to tell her that's not how it was, but she wasn't hearing.

"You ever come near me again, you'll get a knuckle sandwich. And anyway I'm *glad*. Because I never liked you anyway. I just felt sorry for you because you're such a *loser*. And *ugly*!"

She hung up.

October 22

I don't really blame Alvina. If I thought someone be-friended me just because it was her job to do so, I'd be mad too. I keep thinking that the right words, healing words, are out there somewhere, but I can't seem to find them.

O = (BY)422Birch(SE)

October 24

Dootsie is out of control. Her first-grade teacher called Mrs. Pringle today. She said, "If I hear your daughter blurt out, 'I'm gonna be a waffle!' one more time, I'm going to lose my lunch laughing." Mrs. Pringle had to hide the waffle costume so Dootsie won't wear it to school every day.

Dootsie is not 100 percent happy, though. She's miffed that there's nothing for her to win. The parade at school is just that—a parade. Not a contest. No prize for best cos-tume. After her stunning first place at the Blobfest, she craves victories.

"I'm gonna win," she said one day.

"No," I said, "you're not going to win, because there are

no winners. You're just going to walk in the parade with everybody else."

Her face was pouty. "I'm gonna lose?"

"No, you're not going to lose either. There will be no winners, no losers. Only ghosts and witches and goblins. And a waffle."

"A *square* waffle!"

My mother had given her a choice: round or square.

"Yes, a square waffle." I picked her up. "And square waffles everywhere will be counting on you to show the world how wonderful a waffle can be." I kissed her nose. "Can they count on you to do that?"

She rolled her eyes, considering the question. Finally she shrugged and gave a lukewarm, sighful "I guess."

When I take Dootsie around on Halloween night, we'll stay pretty much in her neighborhood. We'll start at Betty Lou's house. And we won't be the only ones visiting that address. I've learned that Betty Lou Fern's is one of the most popular Halloween destinations in town. Her famous agoraphobia draws trick-or-treaters like ghosts to a haunted house. They get a creepy thrill out of stepping onto the porch of a dark dwelling that the inhabitant hasn't left in nine years. They shiver at the possibility that they might get a glimpse of her face. They ring the bell. They knock. They wait. They tremble. But all they ever see is the door open just wide enough for a hand to come out—an almost-old lady's hand—holding a wooden bowl full of donuts cut into halves.

I took a deep breath and called Alvina to ask her to come with us. She hung up as soon as she heard my voice.

It won't surprise me if we run into Perry in our travels. I'm sure he won't pass up this chance to fill a pillowcase with free food.

Oh yes—and Cinnamon will go as a fork.

November 1

I missed Halloween. I missed the last week. Here's what happened:

It was a Wednesday when I wrote to you last. So before sunup next morning, as usual, I headed for Calendar Hill, walkie-talkie in one coat pocket, Cinnamon in the other. As usual, I said goodbye to my mother sitting on the porch. As usual, I passed from glow pool to glow pool as our neighbors' porch lights escorted me down Rapps Dam Road. When I got to the dead end, as usual, I crossed Route 113.

That's when the usual stopped.

I saw flames, off to the right. Even now I don't have the words to describe that moment. The fire. The night. The silence. The solitude. It didn't seem real. It didn't seem *now*. The first thing that popped into my head was: *Lenapes!* Next thing I knew I was yelling into the walkie-talkie: "Mom! Fire! Call 911!" Running and yelling toward the little stucco bungalow: "Fire! Fire! Wake up! Wake up!"

I stepped in a hole. Fell hard. Got up. *Cinnamon! Squashed!* I checked. He was okay. I held him in my hand

and ran. "Wake up! Wake up!" The roof was an orange and yellow blanket of flames, warming my face, lighting the night. The mailbox was bright as midday. White letters on the side said MORNING LENAPE. The little red mail flag was down. Cinnamon's eyes were orange pellets.

What would a fireman do? I ran to the porch. "Wake up! Wake up!" I ran back to the mailbox. I put Cinnamon inside. Closed the metal flap. Opened it—afraid he wouldn't get enough air. I pointed to him. "Stay there!" Back to the porch. "Wake up!" I tried the front door. Locked. Above me the fiery roof sounded like sheets flapping in the wind. The smell was sharp, tarry. Frantically I looked around. Chairs. Wicker. I picked up a chair, pointed the legs at a front window, rammed it into the glass. It bounced back. Flames lit the inside of the house. I could see a grandfather clock. Somewhere a siren was wailing. I rammed the chair again, this time screaming like a karate chopper. The window shattered. I tried to yell, "Wake up!" but I was drowning in smoke. . . .

Next thing I knew there was something over my face. I was looking up into a man's eyes. He was saying, "Just breathe regular. We're giving you oxygen." And then my mother's face, with a look I'd never seen before. I tried to cry out, "Cinnamon!" but my breath was bitter tar. And then the flashing lights . . . the stretcher . . . the siren. . . .

I was in the hospital for a week.

Since they were mainly concerned about my lungs and I was too out of it to complain, it wasn't until later that first night that a nurse pointed and said, "Look." My ankle was like a grapefruit, thanks to the hole I stepped in. Pretty soon it was packed in ice. Then compressed with a felt donut. And elevated above the sheets. And there were cuts on my hands and face from flying glass. And an oxygen tube up my nose. And I was wheezing. And I couldn't talk.

But I could write. I scratched out a note to my parents—they were waiting in the emergency room—telling them where I had put Cinnamon. My dad left and was back in fifteen minutes. He said the mailbox flap was still open but Cinnamon was gone. To tell you the truth, I wasn't surprised. The only time he stays put is when he's with me. He must have run out of patience and got himself down from the mailbox and . . .

The nurse glared. "Stop crying," she said sternly. "You'll gunk up your tubes."

For the first two days I was allowed no visitors but my parents. On the second day my parents finally gave me some good news. No one had been home in the burning house. The owners were at their time-share condo in Florida.

Dootsie and her mother came the third morning. Dootsie wore her waffle costume to cheer me up and because I was going to miss Halloween, but as soon as she saw me she burst into tears. I was still hooked up to oxygen. I still couldn't speak. She tried to pull the tube out; she thought it was hurting me. She asked about Cinnamon. She read the answer in my face. Her mother led her away sobbing. There's nothing sadder than a sobbing waffle.

An hour later Alvina showed up. She hollered at me the whole time. The presence of my parents didn't faze her.

"I thought you were supposed to be smart. But you're not. You're dumb. You're stupid. So don't think you're getting any sympathy from me. It's a good thing you can't talk because you'd probably say something stupid. You tried to break into a house that was on *fire*. To *save* somebody. *And nobody was home!* It doesn't get any stupider than that. The first thing you're gonna say to me when you can talk is, you're gonna say, 'I'm stupid.' If you're not too stupid to understand what I'm saying, nod."

I nodded.

"Okay. Goodbye."

She stomped off.

I guess she's not mad at me anymore.

The Honeybees came. They brought me a pink teddy bear to keep me company. In spite of myself, I find that I like them. Considering that each of them has a one-third stake in the same time-share boy, they seem to get along surprisingly well. They kid each other about who his favorite is. They say I should join them. They say I'd make a great Honeybee. I'm pretty sure they're kidding (*pretty* sure), but I went along with it. I said don't you think the Dandy Man might have something to say about that? They said oh, don't worry, he's already said something.

I thought: *Hmm.*

Next day, Himself showed up. He brought a copy of the *Morning Lenape*, with a front-page story about the fire and a picture of me (school photo from Arizona). The story calls me a "heroic homeschooler." It says the fact that the residents— the Van Burens—were away at the time "does not detract from the valor of the young girl who put her own life in jeopardy to save her neighbors."

I handed it back to him with a sneer. "As Dootsie would say, 'Bullpoopy.' "

His eyebrows went up. "Bullpoopy?"

"I'm no hero. I just happened to be the only one around at that time of night."

We argued about whether I was a hero or not. He won by default, as my sore throat gave out. He was touching a scar on my face when my mother, who had been out of the room, walked in. I introduced them. In the presence of my mother, he suddenly seemed timid. His swagger was gone. I had never seen him be anything but bold before. He patted my teddy bear and left.

Betty Lou has called every day. She's hating herself for not coming to see me, but from the start I ordered her not to. I don't feel I'm the reason she should brave the terror of leaving her house, especially since my condition isn't critical. So we talk and I don't let her hang up until I've persuaded her once again not to feel guilty.

*   *   *

I came home from the hospital this morning. The first thing I did was dump every pebble out of my happy wagon. Empty. Because Cinnamon is gone.

I can't bear to think what happened to him. He's a house rat. He doesn't know about cats and hawks. He doesn't even know there are rat-hating people in the world. I keep seeing him walking up to somebody . . . somebody with big shoes and loathing in his eyes. . . .

I found out they had kept something from me. The day after Dootsie visited me in the hospital, she went missing. She was gone for hours. The police found her near the burned-out house. She was looking for Cinnamon.

I hadn't slept very well those first few nights. They did a blood test and found some toxins from the smoke, so they gave me medicine for that. My airway was constricted, so they gave me medicine for that. I developed a touch of pneumonia—more medicine. My spit was gray—no medicine for that. Gradually things cleared up. They pulled out the oxygen tube, cut back on the pills. Food stopped tasting smoky. My spit is nice and white now.

So my body is doing better, but not my dreams. I see Cinnamon. Sometimes he's wandering a wasteland that looks like the Arizona desert. Señor Saguaro bends down to speak to him, and red-beaked vultures spill out of his elf owl hole. Sometimes Cinnamon is on a crowded sidewalk, dodging shoes, looking up, trying to get someone's attention. Sometimes I don't see him, I only hear him, his voice calling my name over and over.

November 5

The reporter from the *Morning Lenape* came to the house to-day. She's still trying to make me into a hero. She wants to do a profile. I wasn't friendly. I answered two or three questions, then pointed to my throat and croaked, "Can't talk."

She shoved her notebook at me. "You could write your answers."

I shook my head. "Can't write." I grabbed my crutches and hobbled up the stairs to my room and shut the door. I heard her car start up outside. She was probably changing her headline: HEROIC WITCH.

I don't care. My armpits hurt from the crutches. My leg itches under the plastic splint I have to wear whenever I'm not sleeping. I still can't take a deep breath, but even if I could it wouldn't help my heart. I miss my Cinnamon. My littlest friend. I hurt where no crutch or splint can reach.

November 8

I had a fight with my mother last night. (Surprised?) When she found out I intended to go to Calendar Hill this morning, she blew her stack:

"You're not going anywhere! You're still on crutches! You're still wheezing!"

"I am not wheezing," I said calmly, maturely—since she obviously wasn't going to play the part of the grown-up here.

She jabbed her finger in my face. Her cheeks were red. "No."

"Yes."

"No. Debate over."

She turned her back on me and walked away.

"Well, I'm going," I said calmly, maturely.

She stopped. Her shoulders stiffened. She turned. Her eyes were glistening. She said only one word—"Susan"— and turned and walked away.

She never calls me by my first first name unless she's really, *really* upset. At that point I remembered a moment during my second day in the hospital. My parents were in the room. My father was standing, my mother sitting in the chair. They were showing me their cheery faces, daring that old gray spit and wheezing to get me down. Suddenly I started coughing so hard I knocked the IV stand over and practically blew out my oxygen tube. My father ran from the room calling, "Nurse!" A nurse came and got me settled down. When she left and I turned back to my parents, my father was standing directly in front of my mother's chair, so I couldn't see her. He was still smiling and cheery and squeezing my hand. After a minute he moved aside, and there was my mother's face again, smiling and cheery. And now I know clearly what I hadn't known then—my brush with danger had unstrung my parents much more than they had allowed me to see.

Nevertheless . . .

There I was this morning, awake before dawn, thinking

of my neglected calendar, feeling time rushing at me now—43 days till Winter Solstice—and so many things to do. The more I thought about it, the more I persuaded myself that I could sneak out to Calendar Hill and back into bed and my mother would never have to know. I put on my splint, put on my clothes, reached for my crutches—they weren't there. They weren't anywhere in my room. I opened my door, turned on the light, peeked down the hallway, limped to the bathroom. Nowhere. And then it hit me. I limped down to my parents' room, opened the door. There they were, the crutches, snuggled under the covers with my mother. My laughter woke her up. "I'll bet Dad loved this," I said. I climbed in with her, the crutches between us, and we both slept through the sunrise.

November 9

Cinnamon is alive!

Back home!

He's sitting on my shoulder as I write this, nibbling into my ear.

It's a twenty-pebble day!

This morning I was on the sofa, doing the ankle exercises they showed me, when the doorbell rang. Two people stood on the porch. One was Arnold. The other was a woman I didn't recognize. She was dressed smartly in a beige pantsuit and a pale green quilted jacket with a gray fur collar. Her dangling oval earrings were a mosaic of multicolored chips. Her hair was blond with darker streaks. She struck me as someone who is older than she looks. Her smile was dazzling and sure, as if she knew me.

"Stargirl Caraway," she said.

"Yes?"

She thrust out her hand. My right hand was occupied with a crutch, so I shook with my left.

"I'm Rita Wishart." She turned sideways and gestured behind her. "And I think you know my son."

I smiled, nodded. "I do. Hello, Arnold."

Arnold was dressed in his usual moss-green tasseled watch cap and navy peacoat.

"Hello," he said flatly.

It was the first time I ever heard him say something other than "Are you looking for me?"

I invited them in. It was cold outside. Winter is on the way. Standing smiling in the living room, I couldn't imagine why they were here. Arnold was bulky and dark; his mother was tiny and bright.

"Well, I can't stay for but a minute," Rita Wishart said. "I'm semi-retired, but I still do some real estate, and I've got a house to show this morning." She took Arnold's hand and squeezed it. "Arnold has something to show you." Arnold was staring at something over my shoulder. "Arnold."

Arnold reached into a pocket of his peacoat, and when his hand came out it was holding Cinnamon. Cinnamon saw me and leaped onto my chest. He hung on to my shirt with his little nails. I yelped so loud Rita Wishart flinched. I grabbed him in both hands and we nuzzled and cooed shamelessly as if we were alone in the room. At the sound of my voice my mother came running, alarmed. "What happened?" Then she saw Cinnamon, and she went bananas too.

I introduced everyone. Rita told us what had happened:

Early on the morning of the fire, Arnold came walking by. (They live up off Route 113.) A few firemen were still there, dousing the charred, smoking remains. Arnold stopped to watch. He saw the cinnamon-colored rat in the mailbox. He picked it up and took it with him on his day-long, never-ending walk. He took it home and kept it in his room. Next day his mother blew a fuse when she discovered she had a rat in the house. But she quickly calmed down when she saw how clean and friendly it was, not to mention the pretty color. She suspected it was someone's pet—Arnold had simply told her he found it—but she didn't know what to do about it. Put up posters saying FOUND—PET RAT?

And then she read the follow-up story about me in the *Morning Lenape*. She took the clipping from her handbag and showed us. "Haven't you seen it?" she said.

"No," I said.

My mother looked a little sheepish. She said she saw it, then hid it from me. I could see why. The reporter had switched her focus from my "heroism" to my "anguish over the missing pet rat."

"I didn't want to upset you any more than you already were," my mother said.

I glared at my mother. "And *who* told the reporter about Cinnamon?"

My mother raised her hand meekly. "She doesn't give up, that reporter. She called me when you were napping."

I scanned the story. It was surprisingly nice and gentle, considering how nasty I was to the reporter.

"As soon as I read it," said Rita, "I knew who the rat belonged to."

By now my mother and I were practically watering the rug with our happy tears.

"*Please!*" Rita laughed. "You'll get me started. I can't have my mascara running in front of a client. Come on, Arnold."

As they headed for the door, I held out Cinnamon to Arnold. With the tip of his chubby index finger he stroked Cinnamon's head. I handed Cinnamon to my mother and hugged Arnold. He stood stiff as a stone but I didn't care. I pressed my face into the dark wool of his peacoat. I looked into his eyes, which still couldn't seem to find me. "Thank you, Arnold," I said. "If it wasn't for you, Cinnamon would have been an owl's dinner. You saved him."

Rita opened the door. "We're going to the pet shop at the mall tomorrow. We're going to get him his own." She took his hand and led him onto the porch. "Aren't we, Arnold?"

My mother and I and Cinnamon stood in the doorway and watched them go. Then I called Dootsie to tell her the news.

November 13

I'm off the crutches. Off the splint. My ankle color is down to an ugly yellow. I do my exercises every day. Sometimes I still cough when I take a real deep breath. Or laugh. And I've been doing a lot of laughing since Cinnamon came home. I can walk as long as it's not too far. And bike.

I went to Margie's. She had the newspaper story taped in the window.

"Take it down," I told her.

"Mind your own business," she told me. "This is my store."

Neva the new helper wore a beige maternity jumper and looked bigger than ever, if that was possible. She smiled when she saw me and ushered me to a seat and took my jacket off and asked me a million questions about the fire and all. Later I whispered to Margie, "She's not shy anymore." Margie chuckled. "She won't shut up."

Margie forced a dozen donuts on me. Free. "Speed up your recovery," she said.

I visited Betty Lou. We hugged and cried like long-lost sisters.

I pedaled to the cemetery to visit Charlie. Just seeing that red and yellow plaid scarf cheered me up. I had given Betty Lou half the donuts. I handed the rest to Charlie. He put in his hearing aid and shaded his eyes and squinted up at me. "It was you, wasn't it?"

"Me what?"

"In that fire. You were the kid."

I held out my wrists to be cuffed. "Guilty."

He wagged his finger at the gravestone. "See? I told ya. It was the girl with the funny name." He looked up at me. "What's it again? Moon—?"

"Stargirl."

"Yeah, see? Stargirl. I told ya."

He offered me the chair, but I sat on the ground beside him. We talked. Or rather, he talked. About Grace. About how they met when they were six over a fish. In those days there was a fish market where the dollar store is now. They were both there with their mothers. And both mothers wanted the same fish. Charlie remembers it exactly: "It was a halibut. From Alaska." But both mothers were so nice that each insisted the other take it.

"You take it."

"No, you."

Until that moment, they had all been strangers to each other.

While the fishman stood there in his white apron, the mothers kept trying to outnice each other.

"You take it."

"No, you."

Charlie chuckled every time he said this. Even his chuckle was gruff.

Finally, Grace, who was tiny and squeaky, threw both hands in the air and brought the store to a standstill with a thundering bellow: "*I'll* take it!"

As Charlie said this he rose from his chair and threw his hands in the air. The cemetery rang with our laughter.

As he settled back into his chair, wiping the laughter from his eyes, he said, "So Grace's mother got the fish."

I didn't think. I didn't mean to be impertinent or to step on his line. It just came out:

"And you got the girl!"

His head swung to me. The grizzle on his face sparkled like angel fleece. Leo, I have never been smiled at so.

He talked on for hours in that gruff voice of his. He told me he and Grace have a daughter. That's how he gets to the cemetery and back home—his daughter drives him on her way to and from work. He told story after story about him and Grace. They were married at eighteen. Fifty-two years together.

No . . . sixty-four, if you start with the halibut.

No . . . sixty-eight, if you add the time since she came to the cemetery.

Like Neva, Charlie wouldn't shut up. As he jabbered on, I began to understand that he was doing more than talking, more than simply remembering. He was reliving, in a way that can only be done by sharing with someone else. And he was granting me the highest honor of all: he was introducing me to Grace.

When I got up to leave, it was a long time before he let

go of my hand. I took the empty donut bag with me. I wanted to remember the day.

O = (A)431Ringgold(F)

November 15

No fight this time. My mother trundled groggily down the stairs and huddled into the rocking chair on the porch. I put a blanket over her. The days are getting colder.

The porch lights along Rapps Dam Road lit my way to Calendar Hill. The field was especially dark this morning, only a blade of moon showing. I called my mother—"Stargirl has landed. Over and out"—and aimed the flashlight toward the ruins of the Van Burens' house, but it didn't reach. The ground was bumped and crunchy. I was beginning to wish I had brought a crutch.

Caught in the light beam, the almost-completed quarter circle of white spatula paddles seemed otherworldly, like an artifact from aliens or ancient ancestors. I've been numbering the markers with a felt-tip pen. I had gotten up to #15 before the fire. Allowing for the three-week gap, I had #19 in my pocket. I went to the last marker. I knelt beside it. I aimed the light at it, at both sides. Something was wrong. I expected to see #15, but there was no number at all. I looked at the one before. Same thing—no number. Same thing with the next one back. Only when I turned the light on the fourth marker from the end did I see my last number: 16.

What was going on? Had someone been planting markers in my absence? Obviously—but who? *My mother!* I was about to walkie-talkie her when I heard a voice out of the darkness: "Don't homeschool heroes sleep at night?"

Perry.

He walked into the flashlight beam.

"What are you doing here?" I said.

He held up a spatula. "Same thing you are."

I aimed the light at the unnumbered markers. "You did this?"

He shrugged. "Somebody had to."

"You knew how?"

"It's not rocket science."

He turned on his own flashlight. Our beams merged. Time passed. Stars moved.

He laughed.

"What?" I said.

"You. You're standing there with your mouth hanging open, like I have three heads or something."

"I just can't believe you did this. Especially—"

"—since I didn't show up last time?"

"Something like that."

"Long story." He turned off his light. He turned around. "Sky's gray. We better do it."

I turned off my light. He pulled the rope out from the

stake. I handed him my garden trowel, which I bring now that the ground is getting harder. We stood there shoulder to shoulder, looking east. At the first glimmer of sun he dug the hole and I planted my marker. When I stood up my hair brushed his chin, he was so close. Everything was falling at my feet—the trowel, his marker, the rope. And that's when he did it—he kissed me. There on the arc's end of my calendar, on the forty-sixth Thursday of the year, the three hundred and nineteenth morning, thirty-six days till Winter Solstice. Many girls have been romanced under the moon, and I don't mean to say moonlight is overrated, but few I think have known the magic of a sunrise kiss.

We held hands as we walked across the field. At Route 113 we turned in opposite directions and headed for our homes.

November 18

Dear Leo . . .

That's how I was going to start today's entry; then I realized it sounds too much like "Dear John." So scratch that.

It's Sunday afternoon. I'm sitting on the porch with a sweater on. They call a day like this Indian summer. I wonder what the Lenape called it.

I'm looking down the road. I can see just a corner of the field. I can't see the Van Burens' charred ruin. They're allowed to rebuild if they want, but they haven't decided yet. In the meantime, they're living in a trailer in a relative's driveway.

As I sit here on the porch I'm getting a new appreciation of my mother's experience every Thursday morning. She watches me—her daughter, her only child—walk away from her down the corridor of porch lights. She sees me grow dimmer and dimmer until I almost vanish into the darkness beyond the last pool of light—almost, because she still sees the small, reassuring flicker of my flashlight. The flicker swings in her daughter's hand as she crosses Route 113 and onto the field. And then the flicker too disappears as she heads for the calendar. A moment of anxiety, of loss, then the walkie-talkie comes suddenly to life and it's her daughter's voice, perfectly ordinary, no hint of having just flirted with oblivion, her daughter's at-once ordinary and irreplaceable voice saying: "Stargirl has landed. Over and out."

Do I seem like I'm rambling? I am. For three days now I've been rambling, tumbling, skittering, like the leaf I'm watching gust along the street. The gust has been my feelings, and they've been blowing me every which way, and now I think, at last, they have let up and let me settle down to earth and find the words to tell it all. Which, really and simply and finally, is this: I still love you. I don't love Perry.

YOU: I'm surprised.

ME: You're not the only one.

YOU: Considering what you've been saying lately.

ME: I know.

YOU: Care to fill me in?

ME: Well, the most obvious thing is that if you had been here all along, it would have been no contest from the start.

But . . . you are there and he is here, and, as Betty Lou said, I've been lonely and vulnerable. She also told me to inhabit my moments, to live today, to embrace the uncertainty, the mystery of Perry. So I guess that's what I did the other day on Calendar Hill. I plunged into the moment. I let myself drown in it. The setting, the sunrise—talk about a moment! Who could resist? And that moment just went on and on for the rest of that day and into the next. But then I began to notice a funny thing. The moment began to fray at one end and disengage itself from one of its major parts— namely, him, Perry—until there was a clear space between them: the moment here, Perry there. They were *not* one and the same. And I began to feel again something that I had been only dimly aware of before. It was a small, surprising sense of disappointment even as he was kissing me, but the violins were so loud that at the time I could hear nothing else. Now that disappointment was returning, and with it the realization that the magic had come only from the moment, not from him. It was different with you, Leo. In the eyes and ears of my heart, you and the magic are one and the same. The setting never mattered. On the sidewalk in front of my house, at the enchanted place in the desert, walking the halls at school—wherever I was with you, I heard violins.

YOU: Wow. I don't know what to say. I don't deserve you.

ME: You're right, for once.

YOU: After all that, how can I *not* love you back?

ME: Beats me.

YOU: OK, I'm saying it: I love you.

ME: No! I don't want to hear it. Not that way. I never want to hear those words unless they're coming from your lips. The flesh-and-blood you, not the fantasy you.

YOU: I thought you wanted me to say it. You're not making sense.

ME: The heart makes no sense.

YOU: So what *do* you want from me?

ME: The answer is in your question—I want it *from you.* I want you to say the words because they're flying out of your mouth, because you can't possibly stop them, not because I led you to the brink of them. And I want to know that they're being said to me. To *me.* Not to some girl in the movies or a book. Not to some idea of *Girl* that you've picked up along the way from other boys and other girls. To *me.* Stargirl. Do you know *me,* Leo? Really know *me?*

YOU: You're making it hard to say yes.

ME: OK, short course, pay attention . . . Susan Julia Pocket Mouse Mudpie Hullygully Stargirl Caraway 101. She dreams a lot. She dreams of Ondines and falling maidens and houses burning in the night. But search her dreams all you like and you'll never find Prince Charming. No Knight on a White Horse gallops into her dreams to carry her away. When she dreams of love, she dreams of smashed potatoes. She loves smashed potatoes, and she dreams that she and Starboy are eating smashed potatoes, possibly on a blanket at a deserted beach, and as Starboy digs in for another scoopful, he drops the spoon and his mouth falls open (showing some smashed potato goop, but she finds it cute), and he looks at her in a way she's never been looked at before—*he sees her!*—and she can practically see the words boiling up inside him—they're upstoppable!—and here they come, gushing over the smashed potatoes: "I love you, Stargirl!" They just keep coming as potato flecks fly—"I love you, Stargirl! I love you, Stargirl!"—like a cereus blooming not once but over and over a thousand times in a single night.

You understand what I'm saying, Leo?

YOU: You're saying love makes its own magic.

ME: Praise be. There *is* hope.

YOU: I think I'd like to take Stargirl 102.

ME: Stargirl 102 is the same subject matter, but from Starboy's point of view. The lesson is: he must hear violins too, the same ones she hears.

YOU: He did. *I* did.

ME: Maybe so. But you also heard the drumbeat of others. And the drumbeat overpowered the violins.

YOU: I can change.

ME: I hope so.

November 19

I feel panicky. Only 32 days till Solstice and I don't even know what I'm going to do. I wrote to Archie, asking him for ideas. Of course, there's one thing I do know: the central event, the Moment of Moments, will be when the sun peeks over the horizon (pray for clear skies!). I will funnel that light into a hole in a tent—my mother is going to make it—and when it comes out the other side of the hole it will be a single golden spear of light.

But all else is a question. Where shall the golden spear land? There must be a ceremony, but what will it consist of? Who shall I invite? At that time of day, will anybody come?

O = (A)335Ringgold(F)

November 20

I was about to enter Margie's today when I saw Perry inside. He was sitting at the counter, talking to Neva. I kept walking up the street. I'm nervous about seeing him again. What should I say? How does he feel? I don't want to hurt him, but I also don't want to string him along.

The tent will be about the size and shape of my bedroom. My mother has oodles of dry goods connections and she's found this material called Blackbone. It's very tightly woven and coated and, like a dark window shade, it keeps light out. That's what I want. I want it pitch-black inside the tent to dramatically set off the golden sunbeam coming through the hole. My mother says most people with ordinary sewing machines wouldn't be able to work with Blackbone because it's so dense, but her heavy-duty costume-making equipment can handle it. My mother is working from a tent plan drawn up by my father. He will also get poles and stakes from the lumberyard.

Except for a little limp and a scar over one eyebrow—and a tendency to smell tar in unexpected places—my health is back to normal. No small thanks to Dootsie. She keeps brushing my hair and humming homemade tunes to me. Sometimes she shows up with a little white satchel that says DOCTOR. She takes out a toy thermometer and sticks it in my mouth. She listens to my heart with her toy stethoscope; she closes her eyes and nods and murmurs, "M-hm . . . m-hm." She gives me a glass of water and makes me take a pill (peppermint). For a while there, every time she saw me she took off my shoe and sock and gave me a foot massage. Though I surely enjoyed it, I had to put a stop to it the other day when we bumped into the Pringles at the Blue Comet diner and she tried to do it there.

November 21

Tomorrow is Thursday. Calendar Day. And I'm thinking the unthinkable. I'm thinking about not going. Because I'm afraid Perry will be there. I never expected such a complication to interfere with my Solstice routine.

November 22

I went, after all. Because I had a brilliant idea. I called Alvina. I asked her if she could sleep over and go with me in the morning.

"Will it get me out of school?" she said.

"Not really," I said. "There'll be plenty of time to get to school after sunup."

"Then I'm not doing it," she said with a snoot.

I groaned. "All right. You can stay home and hang out with me all day—but only if your mother says so."

When she returned to the phone, she said, "My mom says it's okay. She says it'll be like a field trip."

"Plus if you're with me you won't be getting into trouble."

Alvina snapped, "Hey—how'd you know she said that?"

"I'm psychic."

I only felt a little guilty. Her mother was right—this would be good for Alvina, not to mention give a little more of myself a chance to rub off on her. There was no need for her to know that she would also be running interference for me. If Perry did show up, I figured Alvina's presence would keep things from getting too tense or touchy.

By last night I was regretting the whole thing—and wishing we had a bigger house with a guest room. Alvina slept with me, but she was no out-like-a-light Dootsie. She squirmed and kicked at me all night. I had no sympathy for her as I dragged her out of bed. I had to practically dress her. If it weren't for her anti-Perry value, I would have left her under the covers. It was a sight, my mother and I both wrestling Alvina and trying not to let all three of us go flying down the stairs. Not surprisingly, Alvina wanted to curl up on the porch with my mom, but I dragged her off down Rapps Dam Road as thin snowflakes flurried in the porch lights.

Perry was not at the calendar. I was relieved but still wary. I swung my flashlight beam around. I kept expecting him to come walking out of the darkness, kept expecting to hear his voice. The cold had awakened Alvina as I could not. When she saw the arc of white markers she said, "Cool." I explained the calendar to her. I told her that this was how prehistoric people located themselves in time, in the eternal cycle of the seasons.

I let Alvina pull out the rope. The flurries had stopped. We waited. The sky remained gray with high clouds. The sun, when it rose, was just a smudge, but it was enough. I quick dug the hole and Alvina planted the marker. She tamped the loose dirt with her fist. She coiled the rope back to the croquet stake. She stood there for a while, staring along the new sun line out to our star 93 million miles away. "Cool," she said.

"Give me a minute," I told her. I sat on the cold, clumpy ground. I turned my back on the smudgy sunrise so that I was facing west, facing you. I closed my eyes and I did something I've been thinking about: I sent you a message. A question. I hope you receive it.

Then I got up and we left.

*   *   *

Later, I took Alvina to Betty Lou's for lunch. As I was about to ring the doorbell, Alvina said, "I'm not going in there."

"Why?" I said.

"Because she's a witch."

"Who said that?"

"Everybody."

"You listen to *everybody*? Doesn't sound like you, Miss Don't-Mess-With-Me."

"She didn't leave this house for years and years. Her face is all white and dusty, like chalk. She never opens the windows. There's mold and slime all over. And cooties. It's disgusting."

"If it's so disgusting, how come you bring her donuts every week?" I said, and rang the bell.

The door opened at once. Alvina flinched back. A hand came out and a crooked finger waggled to us and a creaky, creepy voice leered, "Come in, my children."

I laughed. Alvina squawked and headed for the sidewalk. I grabbed the tail of her jacket and pulled her back and dragged her into the house. I stood behind her and wrapped my arms around her and made her face Betty Lou, who was her usual magnificent self in purple bathrobe and bright red slipper socks. "Betty Lou," I said, "this is—"

Betty Lou interrupted, "I know who it is. The pip. Alvina. My donut angel."

She held out her hand. Alvina put hers in her pockets. I snapped, "Alvina!" but Betty Lou laughed out loud. "That's okay. I wouldn't shake the hand of somebody with cooties either."

I boggled. "You heard?"

"I saw you coming. I was at the door, listening." She nodded thoughtfully. "Very interesting. So, Alvina, what else do they say about me?"

Alvina mumbled, "Nothin'."

"Oh come on, Alvina. Don't be such a wuss. If you don't tell me, I'll shake my hair and cooties will fly all over you."

Alvina backed tighter into me. "There's a dead body upstairs. You sleep with it. It's your husband that died forty years ago."

Betty Lou's eyebrows went up. "I'm impressed. Seems I'm much more interesting than I ever realized." She headed for the kitchen. "Well, come on in, you two. I have some cootie buns for you."

I kept hold of Alvina's hand till we were seated at the kitchen table. Betty Lou brought out a treat I had never seen before. "Homemade sticky buns. Yum yum." She passed the tray before Alvina's nose. "And your choice—raisins or pecans."

"Go ahead, take two," I said.

"I'm not hungry," said Alvina.

"Alvina—" I took her head in my hands and swiveled it around the kitchen. "Do you see mold and slime anywhere?"

Betty Lou play-slapped my hand. "Oh, let her be. If she's hungry, she'll eat. Nothing worse than being forced to eat, especially homemade sticky buns. Right, Alvina?"

Alvina glanced at the tray of buns. She nodded.

"In fact," said Betty Lou, "I think I'll warm them in the microwave. Warm sticky buns? Raspberry Zinger tea? Yum-*eee*." She squeezed Alvina's stunned face in her hand and put on a down-home accent: "Honey, it don't git no better'n this."

Soon the smell of homemade sticky buns filled the kitchen. She made Raspberry Zinger tea for herself and me. As she laid the warm tray of buns on the table, she made sure to pass it by Alvina's nose. I was gagging on chuckleballs.

"So," said Betty Lou, sitting down, "you can go upstairs if you want, see the body."

Alvina shrugged. "That's okay." Then she looked straight at Betty Lou. "How come you never leave the house?"

Betty Lou's finger shot into the air. "Ah, the inquisition." She eyed Alvina slyly. "Okay, Donut Damsel, here's the deal. You agree to eat one sticky bun—and I'll spill the beans. I'll tell you everything you want to know. I'll confess. I'll squeal." She held out her hand. "So, is it a deal?"

This time Alvina shook. As Betty Lou told the story— "The Abominable Agoraphobic," she called it—including chapters on her reign as Dogwood Blossom and stuff even I had never heard, Alvina polished off the whole tray of sticky buns and three cups of Raspberry Zinger.

November 23

Day by day the voice that started as a tiny whisper has become louder and louder until this morning it woke me out of my sleep:

**HE HASN'T TRIED TO CONTACT YOU SINCE
THAT DAY. IT'S BEEN MORE THAN A WEEK. GUESS
WHAT? MAYBE IT'S MUTUAL. MAYBE HE
DOESN'T LOVE YOU EITHER.**

It comes as a shock. I feel:

a. Embarrassed (that it took me so long to see it)

b. Embarrassed, the sequel (for believing I was the only one not in love)

c. Insulted (how can he *not* love me?)

d. Relieved

e. Curious (what happens next?)

November 24

Today I got the phone call I've been looking forward to for months. It was Betty Lou, squealing with joy:

"I have a mockingbird! Up on the telephone wire out back! Listen! I'll hold the phone out!" I heard a window go up. I heard faint birdsong. "Hear?"

"I do," I said.

"I'm so happy! My own mockingbird! I'm terrified it's going to leave!"

"Try putting a sliced orange outside," I said. "I hear they like that." I thought of her problem. "Just toss it into the backyard. He'll find it."

"I will! I will!" Then a pause, a shriek. "I have no oranges!"

"I'll bring some over."

"Hurry!"

Had you guessed, dear Leo, what the mysterious equations were about? I lured the mockingbird from street to street, block to block, with oranges until we reached 335 Ringgold—Betty Lou's address. Don't ever tell her. I want her to think this is strictly between her and the mockingbird.

Days till Solstice: 27

November 25

I heard back from Archie yesterday. He says forget about history. Don't worry about making my Solstice conform to descriptions in books. For thousands of years every culture and country and age has done Solstice its own way—why should I be any different? They're all based on the same sun, the same earth, the same special dawning. It's about time turning a corner. It's about knowing that warm days will return, that there will be another planting, another harvest. It's about rejoicing. It's about people together. He underlined it: <u>together.</u>

The Perry Suspense is getting to me. Before, I was trying to avoid him. Now I'm antsy. I just want to get our next encounter out of the way so we can get on with whatever comes next.

November 26

So I rode my bike past the high school as the students were leaving. I didn't see him. (I don't know what I would have done if I did.) I went downtown. I checked in Margie's. No Perry.

"And you can say goodbye to Neva," said Margie. "This is her last day." Neva was right beside us, wiping donut trays, but she was as quiet and somber as the first time I met her. Margie reached out and patted Neva's tummy. There was a hint of sadness in her smile. "Baby time."

Neva's highlighted hair and glittery earrings seemed to mock her mood. When I said, "Congratulations, Neva," she only nodded.

Don't-know-when-to-stop me, I tried a question: "Do you know if it's a boy or girl?"

"Girl," she muttered. Hard to believe this was the person who talked my head off two weeks ago.

"That's nice," I said brilliantly. I needed an escape remark. I added, "Well, it'll be a nice Thanksgiving present," and headed for the door.

Back outside, I resumed my search for Perry. I walked up and down Bridge Street. I bumped into two of the Honeybees. They tried to drag me into Pizza Dee-Lite, but I said I had somewhere to go. I rode over the canal to Perry's place. I circled around Ike's Bike & Mower Repair. I did everything but stop and knock on the back door. I rode home— mission unaccomplished—

And bumped into Perry on my front porch.

With Dootsie.

I parked my bike. Dootsie jumped into my arms.

"We were just looking for you," he said. "Your mother said you were out, she didn't know where."

He was blushing. I had never seen that before.

"Just cruising," I said. "Giving my ankle a workout."

I felt his blue eyes on me, but I kept mine on Dootsie. She was fingering my eyebrow scar. A few days ago I had brought Alvina to Calendar Hill with me for protection. I wondered if Perry was using Dootsie the same way.

"So . . . hanging out with first-graders, huh?" I said.

He chuckled, shrugged. His usual breezy glibness was gone. He was uneasy.

Dootsie tapped my nose. "He likes you."

I tapped her nose. "Of course he likes me. And I like him. That's what friends do, they like each other."

She wagged her head. "No, silly. I don't mean *that*. I mean"—she cupped her hands and whispered in my ear—"he likes you for a *girl*friend."

"Oh really?" I was wondering how to turn this conversation in another direction when my father's milk truck pulled into the driveway. He came out with an armload of tent poles and stakes. He clattered past us into the house and was back on the porch in a minute, scowling at me.

"Well, Miss Hospitality, there's already two things you didn't do. You didn't introduce me to your friend"—he nodded at Perry—"and you didn't ask them to come in out of the cold."

"I'm her friend too," Dootsie protested.

My father took her from me. "You need no introduction. You're famous."

I introduced my father to Perry and invited them into the house. Sometimes life goes its own way and drags you along.

As soon as Dootsie took off her winter coat she pulled up her shirt and yelped, "Look!"

My heart sank. It was a tattoo. Black and yellow. A honeybee. On her little belly proudly bulging.

I glared. "Really, Perry, this is taking robbing the cradle to a new low."

Perry was all flustered innocence. "Hey—she *wanted* it. I made her ask her *mother*. It washes off. No big deal."

Dootsie fished into her pants pocket and came out with a paper tattoo. She thrust it in front of me. "For you!"

"No, thank you," I said, still glaring at Perry. "I don't do dandelions. Or harems."

It was written all over Perry's face: *This was a bad idea.* He repeated weakly, "It washes off."

"Right," I said, taking the tattoo from Dootsie and flipping it over to him, "but not everything washes off, Mr. Delloplane."

I'm not even sure what I meant by that, but it sounded good. And then my mother was trailing cooking smells into the living room and inviting the two of them to join us for dinner, and I wanted to shout, *No!* but instead found myself telling Dootsie to call and ask her mother.

For dinner we had spaghetti and meatballs—veggie-burger balls for me. Dootsie kept my parents in stitches.

My father drove Dootsie and Perry home—Dootsie insisted they ride in the milk truck, not the car. As my mother and I cleaned up the dinner table, she said, "So . . . Perry . . ."

"Mm."

"Boyfriend?"

"Not really."

"No?"

"No. I thought he might be. Might become. But no."

"So . . . what?"

"Friend. I think. I hope. Once I get over being mad at him. He's a pretty neat guy."

"And Leo?"

"Leo's still"—I nodded toward the window—"there." I patted my chest. "Here."

She smiled, kissed me. "I'm glad Dootsie's in your life."

"Me too."

"Little sister you never had."

I nodded. I didn't trust my voice.

November 27

I need a break from the Perry thing. I went to see Charlie at the cemetery. He was nodding off in his chair. As I was walking my bike away I heard, "Hey!"

"Didn't want to wake you," I said.

He inserted his hearing aid. He pulled his thermos from under the chair. He twisted off the red plastic cup, thrust it at me. "Hot chocolate."

"No thanks," I said.

He pulled a second cup from his pocket. This was new. He held it out. "Come." It was an order.

"Okay."

He poured us both some. He pulled a blanket out from under the chair. This was new also. He already had a blanket over his legs. He didn't need another. He laid it beside the chair and unfolded it once. "Sit."

We talked about small things. Somewhere along the way I said, "I'd like to hear about you when you were little. Before Grace. Just Charlie."

He blinked at me. I could see him making the effort. He gazed at the tombstone. He shook his head, gave up trying. "Ain't no before Grace."

As if to confirm, a large crow settled boldly onto a head-stone only several plots away, cawed once loud and rudely, and flew off.

I invited Charlie to come to Thanksgiving dinner with us. We're going to Betty Lou's. He said no, he'd rather stay here. He said his daughter will pack him a turkey dinner to bring along. It will include Grace's masterpiece: sweet potato casserole with marshmallow topping. He grinned, wagging his head. "Won't be the same, though. She knew how to do the marshmallows just right. Singe 'em. Brown, not black. Just crusty enough." He closed his eyes. He was tasting it.

November 28

I was pedaling along Route 113 today when I saw Arnold. He had his new pet rat. On a leash! They were on the other side of the road. I practically crashed into a telephone pole. I stopped and stared. The rat was gray and white. What they call a hooded rat, because the gray covers its face and comes down over its shoulders. Someone—probably Arnold's mother—had worked up a tiny harness (a collar wouldn't do on a rat) and an ordinary dog-type leash. The rat was scooting along after him. Arnold's shuffle seemed a little slower than usual. I finally started up again and wobbled giggling all the way into town.

Days till Solstice: 23

November 29

Thanksgiving Thursday for me began at Calendar Hill. Since he wasn't working on the holiday, my father took over sit-on-the-porch-and-keep-an-eye-on-Stargirl duties. For a milkman, getting up a little before sunrise must feel like sleeping in.

I was less anxious about Perry this time. I didn't really expect him to be there. He wasn't. It was so cloudy there wasn't even a hint of sun, so I had to guess about the marker placement. I stepped back to look at the arc of white markers. If time has to be measured, this is the way to do it. I felt a tingle of excitement. Only three more to go.

As I did last week, I sat facing west and sent you my message. I'll do it every week from now on.

Betty Lou was a wonderful Thanksgiving hostess. No bathrobe on this day. She looked like a regular person in a skirt and sweater—well, regular if you don't count the turkey headdress pinned to her hair. "I've worn it every Thanksgiving since I was six," she said.

She made everyone, including Cinnamon, sit in the kitchen while she bustled about and asked my father a hundred questions about being a milkman and my mother about costume making. She was so chatty and breezy that when she said, stirring the giblet gravy, "You know, Mr. and Mrs. Caraway, your daughter and Dootsie are my lifeline," I almost missed it. My mother reached for my hand and squeezed.

At the festive dinner table, printed name cards told us where to sit. Yes, there was a card for Cinnamon and a tiny antique dollhouse saucer with three candied cranberries. For Cinnamon's vegetarian mother there was tofurkey, for everyone else turkey, and cheese-and-garlic smashed potatoes for all. It took us hours to eat because we spent so much time laughing. Betty Lou turned from inquisitor to storyteller. She re-created hilarious scenes from her school days and made fun of her agoraphobia and even lampooned her disastrous one and only marriage to Mr. Potato Nose. At one point my mother laugh-snorted coffee out her nose.

Later, in the living room, the mood mellowed. Betty Lou enthralled my parents with her tale of the night-blooming cereus (back in the living room for the winter, thanks to her neighbor Mr. Levanthal) and the moonlit hours she shared with me. It was chilly in the house—Betty Lou left a back window open, "the better to hear my mockingbird." Twice she held up her finger and whispered, "Let's just listen," and we sat there smiling, eyes closed, as the mockingbird entertained us and cups of hot mulled cider warmed our hands.

It was the best Thanksgiving I've ever had.

December 3

I think of you in your college. I wonder how many room-mates you have. You'll be interested to know that your college is on the same latitude as my Pennsylvania town. Of course, you are still well to the west of me, but weather travels from west to east, and it's nice to know that the rain and snow that falls on you in a day or two will fall on me.

I sat down today and started writing out the guest list. I was shocked at how many. I asked my mother if the tent could be made bigger. She said no, there's not enough time to order more Blackbone.

I've put Dootsie and Alvina to work. I went to a crafts store and bought sheets of bright yellow foam and a bunch of bar pins. Then I made a sunburst pattern out of cardboard and gave everything to the girls. Dootsie's job is to trace the patterns onto the yellow foam, then Alvina cuts out the sunbursts. Dootsie keeps begging to do the cutting, but Alvina has orders not to let her near the scissors. Alvina keeps complaining about Dootsie's sloppy tracing.

Days till Solstice: 18

December 5

Again I saw Arnold walking his rat, only this time I did something that surprised even me. I got off my bike and started walking along with him. I said hi. He said hi. I asked him the name of his rat. He said, "Tom."

"Nice name," I said.

"Are you looking for me?" he said.

It was as if I were hearing his eternal question for the first time. *Was* I looking for him? Had I been looking for him all along and didn't know it? What if I said yes? How would he react? I peered into his grizzled face. His eyes seemed empty, unfocused, but I knew that was not true. They were simply seeing another place, another time.

"I'm not sure, Arnold," I said. "Let me get back to you on that."

And then, surprising myself again, I started talking. I hadn't planned to. The words just came gushing out. I started off talking about the Perry Problem. The Kiss. Stuff I hadn't said to Betty Lou or my parents or even Archie. But pretty soon I veered away from Perry and on to you. Us. I told him about the First Day, when Kevin said, "Why him?" and I tweaked your earlobe and said, "Because he's cute." I recounted every moment of the First Night, when I came outside and you hid behind the car and I let Cinnamon loose to visit you and we had the sweetest conversation I've ever had in my life, me on the front step, you crouching behind the car, unseen to each other. Later, on the same sidewalk, the First Kiss. The Forever Kiss.

On and on I gabbed to Arnold. I think I had discovered that the closest I could come to reliving the past was to tell my story to someone, the right someone.

It was wonderful, the telling, the going back. When I returned to the present, Tom was on Arnold's shoulder and we were on the other side of town. I climbed on my bike. I coasted beside him for a minute.

"Arnold?" I said. He didn't respond. "I think the answer is yes. Yes, I was looking for you. I'm glad I found you."

Arnold gave no sign of having heard me. I stayed behind as he shuffled on out of town. Tiny puffs of frosty air came from Tom's nose.

December 6

The earth at Calendar Hill is really hard now and cold. I had to punch through with a screwdriver to plant today's marker. Only two more markers to go. Two more Thursdays. Two more chances to send my question to you.

Sudden thought: *What if it's cloudy on Solstice and there's no sun? What if it snows? What if the snow is so deep it covers the paddles?*

"Sun schmun," said my mother.

"Snow schmow," said my dad. *"Qué será, será."*

"Spanish?" I said.

"Yeah," he said. "Means don't sweat the small stuff."

Alvina and Dootsie are into phase 2 of their job: attaching the self-stick bar pins to the backs of the sunburst buttons. Dootsie keeps missing the centers of the buttons. Alvina keeps telling Dootsie she's fired, but Dootsie knows I'm the real boss, so she just sticks out her tongue at Alvina and goes on making a mess.

Days till Solstice: 15

December 10

The town is in a tizzy. Or at least you'd think so if all you did was read the *Morning Lenape*.

Here's what happened:

Every Christmas season Grace Lutheran Church erects a nativity scene on the lawn out front. The figures are life-size, the barn plenty big enough for Joseph, Mary, and the manger and cows and sheep. The straw is real. You can smell it. From the street you can't see the doll that represents Jesus, but you can see the sky-blue blanket falling over the sides of the manger. With the spotlights, even on the coldest nights the scene seems warm and cozy. Cars going past slow down. Some stop.

Last Friday the church secretary discovered that the blanket in the manger was gone. The baby Jesus doll was naked on the bed of straw.

CRECHE VANDALIZED;
DOLL LEFT IN COLD

read the headline in the *Morning Lenape*.

Today's paper did a "From the Sidewalk" segment, where passersby are asked about a burning local issue of the day.

One person said, "It's an outrage. Isn't anything sacred anymore?" Another said, "When they find out who did it, they should put him in jail and throw away the key." And another: "This is a black eye for the whole town." And another: "Hey, it's not really Jesus. It's a *plastic doll*. Hello? Get a life."

I'm pretty sure I know who did it. But I can't figure out why.

Meanwhile, the manger has a new blue blanket.

DTS: 11

December 11

The long-range weather forecast says it's going to snow on December 21—Solstice. Indians in the Old West did rain dances. I called Dootsie and Alvina over and we did a no-snow dance. Dootsie went wild. At first Alvina said it was "stupid," but five minutes after Dootsie and I stopped, she was still going.

My father keeps trying to calm my weather anxiety. He said even if it's too cloudy to see, the sun will still rise, it will still be there.

"But that's the whole point," I said. "*Seeing* it."

"Is it?" he said.

DTS: 10

December 12

The town tizzy has gone the way of all tizzies: it fizzled. But I still think about it. I still wonder why.

DTS: 9

December 13

I planted the sunrise marker at the calendar this morning. One more marker to go. One more chance to send you the question.

Later I saw Perry walking downtown. Nothing unusual about that, just another one of his "sick days," except . . . *he was pushing a baby carriage!* I nearly crashed my bike into a curb.

We stared at each other. He looked perfectly normal, like this happened every day. He also looked different— new, older. My first thought was: *He's a father!*

Then: *Which Honeybee is the mother?*

Then: *So why was he putting the moves on me?*

At long last he laughed. "You should see your face."

I mumbled out something I don't even recall.

"Well," he said, turning the carriage so I could see the face of the sleeping baby, "meet Clarissa. My sister." He pulled a doll-size arm out from under the blanket—*the sky-blue blanket*—and waved a tiny hand at me and said in a peepy voice, "Hi, Stargirl."

Tears filled my eyes. I waved back. "Hi, Clarissa." I hope I smiled. Slowly my wits were returning. "How old?"

The answer came at once, without calculation. "Twenty-two days, seven hours."

I reached out. I stroked the tiny fingers. "You never said."

He just shrugged. He returned her hand to the blanket. Passersby were slowing down, peering into the carriage, smiling. A few glanced at Perry, at me.

"Perry—" I said, just to fill the awkward silence, when suddenly something clicked into place. Followed by more somethings clicking into place. Baby blanket . . . pregnant lady . . . Perry in Margie's with . . .

"Perry—" I stammered. "Neva? . . . From Margie's? . . . Oh my God . . . is she . . . your *mother*?"

He smiled. He pistol-pointed at me. "Bingo."

I must have stared like a moron for an hour. A thousand questions clamored, but in the end all I said was, "Nice blanket."

He looked at it, gave an impish grin, knowing I knew. "Yeah."

"Got to have a nice warm blanket for a new baby sister to keep her warm on cold winter days, right?"

He walked off, called back, "You said it."

It took Margie a full minute to finish laughing. *"Jail?"* she repeated. *"Boot camp? Criminal?"* And she sat on a counter stool and laughed some more. "Who told you *that*?"

I pushed an answer past my stupidity and embarrassment: "Alvina."

"Well," she said, "you should have asked me. He was off with an aunt in Scranton. Making money to help his mother. Had himself three jobs." She wagged her head. "Boot camp."

For the next hour Margie filled me in on the Life of Perry Delloplane:

He came back from Scranton because his mother—Neva—missed him too much.

His mother suffers from depression. Hence the mood swings. She takes medicine for it.

His mother has an incurable weakness for his father, whose name is Roy.

Roy has an incurable weakness for gambling. Roy gambled away all their money at the casinos in Atlantic City. Then he got loans from sharks that he couldn't pay back, and the sharks came after him for their money and he took off for good. This was when Perry was five.

Except Roy doesn't always stay away. Every now and then, when he feels like it, he comes knocking. And much to Perry's displeasure, Neva always lets him in.

Roy is baby Clarissa's father.

Not Ike. Ike lets them stay behind his repair shop for free. He gets to be Neva's boyfriend when Roy isn't around.

Perry hates Roy. When Roy stays overnight, Perry sleeps on the roof. Not because it's too hot in the house.

And Margie told me there's something even Perry doesn't know: he thinks he's stealing, but in many cases he's the only one who thinks so. Some of the merchants downtown are aware of Perry's situation—"thanks to my big mouth," says Margie with a laugh—and they make a point of looking the other way when they see him reaching for a lemon, a notebook, a bar of soap.

Like me, Margie knew who had taken the blue blanket as soon as she heard about it.

DTS: 8

December 15

My poor fingers. I spent all of yesterday handwriting the invitations. The guest list includes just about everyone I've mentioned in this endless letter. If they all come, the tent won't hold them. But that will never happen. Why did I ever make so many buttons?

Here's what the invitation says:

Come To A Celebration
of
WINTER SOLSTICE!
Rte. 113 and Rapps Dam Road
December 21
Before **Sunrise!!!**

I've decided not to call it Solstar, as Perry suggested on the roof that night. Who am I to change its name?

DTS: 6

December 17

I spent most of the last two days delivering invitations. Alvina and Dootsie helped. My father too, on his milk route.

When I handed Charlie his invitation at the cemetery, he read it and handed it back to me and said, "I gotta be here." I stuffed the paper into his pocket. I leaned down from my bike and kissed him on the cheek. I reached into his pocket and got the hearing aid and inserted it and whispered into that ear: "She won't be *here* that day. She'll be *there*." I rode off.

It was almost dark when I delivered the last of the invitations. I pedaled up the bluff overlooking the old steel plant, to the spot where legend says the Lenape maiden leaped to her death. With a whisper of apology to Perry for violating my own anti-litter beliefs, I set her invitation on the ground and rode home.

DTS: 4

December 18

I kept to myself all day. As the time draws near, I feel the need to be alone, to get myself ready. I've composed a song, to be accompanied by ukulele. I will just pluck an occasional string—no strumming. I'm working on a dance. I've made a red and yellow wreath of bittersweet berries to frame the sun spot. I've written some words.

Still, I have the sense that something is missing, that I'm overlooking something.

The only person I'm tempted to visit is Betty Lou. I'm dying to know if she's coming to Solstice, if she'll leave her house for the first time in nine years. But I don't want to put pressure on her. If she comes, it should be of her own free will.

I'm trying to ignore the fact that it's snowing in Chicago.

DTS: 3

December 19

I'm afraid nobody will show up. Well, not exactly nobody. I know Dootsie and Alvina will be there. And my parents. And Margie. And Cinnamon. But I'm not sure about anybody else.

I've rehearsed the song.

And the dance.

And the words.

It's snowing in Pittsburgh.

DTS: 2

December 20

Except for putting up the tent, I expected today to be mostly a day of seclusion and contemplation, the soul's quiet preparation before the big event.

It didn't turn out that way.

Because today happens to be a Thursday, my mother staggered down the stairs before sunrise, muttering, "One last time . . . one last time . . . ," and for one last time she sat on the rocking chair and watched me trek down the aisle of frosty porch lights to Calendar Hill.

Only my flashlight lit the field on this moonless, cloudy night. For one last time I pulled the rope out from the croquet stake and planted the final marker. A dismal daylight came, but not the sun. Ninety-three million miles the sunlight traveled only to be blocked by clouds shrouding this hill on planet Earth. And so my final paddle placement, the most important placement of all, is imperfect. All I could do was eyeball the long arc of markers stretching from July to December and take my best guess at where the last one should go.

I hate having to resort to guesswork. If my paddle placement is off, the whole thing is going to flop. The setup will be like those pinhole cameras for indirectly viewing an eclipse. The light from the rising sun—*Please let there be a rising sun tomorrow*—will strike the front panel of the Blackbone tent. The light will funnel through a little round hole in the panel and will fly through the tent as a golden sunbeam. It will land as a circular spot of sunlight—the Solstice Moment—on the back, black panel, hopefully in the center of the bittersweet wreath. But if the alignment of the tent-hole-to-backdrop is off, the sunbeam will miss the mark and go flying off to Route 113 and beyond, and we will all be staring at a black, blank wall.

I sat down on the ground and closed my eyes, but I couldn't get the weather and the paddle placement problem out of my head. My mind wash was a washout. When I finally gave up and opened my eyes, my upturned palms were wet from the first snowflakes. I turned west to send my final weekly message to you, my question, but I was so distracted I'm afraid it was garbled.

So much for quiet contemplation.

My father hurried through his milk route today, so that by early afternoon I was back on the hill helping him set up the tent. The snow was already up to our shoe tops. Off at the edge of the field the charred remains of the Van Burens' house were turning white.

We footed snow away and dug four pole holes. My father used a heavy hammer and a screwdriver to break the frozen ground. We pulled up the croquet stake, and that's where the back wall of the tent went.

There were five panels of Blackbone material: four walls and the roof. They were heavy and totally impervious to light. My mother had folded over the edges to resist tearing and had fitted the pole and stake rope holes with brass reinforcement rings. I don't know how her sewing equipment managed to punch through that material.

I myself can hardly build a sandwich, much less a tent, so I was only too happy to be a working grunt while my dad gave the orders. Plus, with the snow falling fat and furry, I worked to keep myself from bawling over the weather.

"It's a fast-moving storm," my father kept saying. "It'll be clear by tomorrow."

I didn't believe him.

I picked a spot on the front, east-facing panel, straight up from today's marker. Using a cardboard cutout I had made at home, I traced a circle on the Blackbone with a yellow marker. A small circle, about the size of a golf ball. My father cut the hole out. He squeezed some plastic stuff around it so the edge wouldn't fray. The sharper the circle, the better the sunbeam.

The last thing I did was pull up the markers. They had done their job. They had led us to the spot.

*   *   *

It was getting dark by the time we climbed into the milk truck for the short ride home. In the driveway my father said, "You go in. I'm going to shovel." Which struck me as odd, because he teases our next-door neighbor Mr. Cantello about the folly of bringing out his shovel before snow has stopped falling. But I was in no mood for debate.

The moment I opened the front door I smelled it, the scent I would know anywhere: cherry pipe tobacco. I screamed, "Archie!" and ran for the kitchen lights. There he was at the table with my mother, both of them grinning at me. I squeezed him until he begged for mercy. My pent-up emotions about tomorrow came gushing as tears of joy. I nuzzled my nose into his new white beard, which by now must be old stuff to you.

Archie told me he had decided long ago to attend my Solstice. My parents had conspired with him to keep it a surprise. The first thing he noticed was that I wasn't wearing my fossil necklace as a member in good standing of the Loyal Order of the Stone Bone. I told him I had surrendered it to a good cause on April Fools' Day. "I'll send you another," he said. He squeezed my hand. "Señor Saguaro sends his regards"—and the lingering unsettlement of my cactus dreams vanished.

We never left the kitchen. My parents sat with us for a while, then went to bed. Cinnamon meandered about the table, nosed into the tobacco pouch, and finally curled up to sleep on a place mat.

Archie loved looking at the kitchen wall and finding no clock there. "My kind of house," he said. "I'm stuck back in the Carboniferous, anyway." And he tossed his wristwatch into the wastebasket.

He brought me up-to-date on happenings in Mica. He told me about the Ocotillo Ball last spring. "They did your bunny hop," he said, "right off the tennis courts and into the darkness of the golf course. But they tell me it wasn't the same without you. You're becoming a kind of legend in those parts."

I waggled my fingers and ghosted my voice: "Ooooh . . . the mysterious visitor who came and went."

He laughed. "Don't overrate yourself. Let me do that."

I struck a melodramatic pose. "When you speak of me, Professor, tell them, 'She is just an old-fashioned girl.'"

He laid his hand on mine. He smiled and nodded. "More than you know, my dear."

I think he was opening a door for me, but I wasn't ready to go in.

We talked and talked. Then, somewhere along the line, I became aware that the conversation had stopped and that Archie was staring at me with an imp in his eye.

"What?" I said.

He tamped tobacco into his pipe bowl and set another round of cherries on fire. "It's not like you."

I was confused. "What's not?"

"Dishonesty."

As Betty Lou would say, befuddled. "Huh?"

"By your standards, anyway." He stroked sleeping Cinnamon. "Not like you to think or feel something for so long and not express it."

Uh-oh.

I just stared at him for five or six eternities. I put out a wincey peep: "I'm scared."

He drew on his pipe and produced two gray, puffed words: "Don't be."

I took a deep breath. "Okay, I'll ask . . . What about Leo?"

His smile erased my fears. "Leo," he said—and it thrilled me just to hear him pronounce your name—"is fine. He talks about you . . . more than fossils!" We laughed at that. "He misses you. He's maturing. He's beginning to show signs that one day he may even deserve you."

He told me what I already knew from Dori Dilson, that you went with Dori to the Ocotillo Ball, not as boyfriend and girlfriend but as "friends of Stargirl." He told me that you and Dori speak of going to Phoenix one day next summer, where you'll stop and eat at the first silver lunch truck you come to.

He told me you're home from college now on your holiday break. He said you're thinking of majoring in design. He said there are days when you just can't go off to class without wearing the porcupine necktie I gave you.

I was ravenous for information. I squeezed every drop I could out of Archie, squeezed him dry till he was nothing but rind. Which was when he raised his hand and said, "Okay—enough of that boy. What about tomorrow?"

I showed him the guest list. "Wow," he said. "Anybody *not* invited?"

"It's everybody whose name I know," I told him. "And some I don't."

His finger traced a name. "Dootsie. Your little friend?"

"My best friend. She's six."

He nodded, not surprised. I told him about Dootsie and Alvina and Betty Lou and Charlie and Arnold. I was going to update him about Perry and me—but I chickened out.

"I'm afraid nobody will come," I said. "I'm afraid half won't come because they don't care, and the snowstorm will keep the rest away—including the sun. And even if there *is* a sunrise, I'm afraid it's going to miss the target because I messed up the last marker."

He stared at me for a while, then said, "Finished?"

I nodded.

He wagged his head and chuckled.

"Thanks for your support," I said. I got up from my chair.

"Where are you going?" he said.

"Porch. Check the snow."

"Don't."

The way he said it, I stopped. I sat back down.

He looked at me across the table. "Silly worries don't become you. Did I ever tell you about my pet peeve?"

"No," I said.

"People who dress up their pets to look like Little Lord Fauntleroys or cowboys, clowns, ballerinas. As if it's not enough just to be a dog or cat or turtle. Dressing up nature." He spat smoke. "Bushwah."

"*Bushwah?*"

"Profanity. Origin unknown."

His eyes bored into mine, willing his meaning into me. I

can be pretty dense sometimes, but it was beginning to sink in. By the time I lay down to sleep, I was at peace. Archie has always had that effect on me. Just hearing him speak of you was the next best thing to having you at the kitchen table too— maybe, for now, even better. My anxiety about the weather had fled. And I had come to a decision about tomorrow.

DTS: 1

December 23

It's over.

It will never be over.

Two mornings have already passed since then. They just don't stop coming, do they?

Archie walked to the hill with me and Cinnamon under the Solstice stars—yes, the sky was clear! Snow lay over the earth like piled moonlight. My parents were already there. My mother was knocking snow off the roof panel with a broom— "It was sagging bad"—and my father was slicing through a side panel with a box cutter. "What are you *doing?*" I said.

"I saw your guest list on the kitchen table," he said. "No way you were going to fit them all inside." So he was cutting out the two side panels of Blackbone, so there wouldn't be an "inside" for people to be left out of. I was tempted to say we'd be lucky to fill half the tent, but I didn't.

Archie's pipe flared: firelight on moonlight on snowlight. "Could read a book out here tonight," he said.

"If the night's not dark," I said, "how can we have a proper sunrise?"

He scowled at me. "There you go again, worrywart."

"Sorry." I smacked my hand.

My father was nearly finished cutting out the side panels when we heard a voice: "Stargirl!"

I didn't have to look. "That," I told Archie, "would be Dootsie."

In the distance silhouetted figures were moving across the snow. Two of them, adult-size, were walking, one pulling a sled. On the sled was a huddled shape that I assumed must be Dootsie—except that it was too big to be just her. Then the huddled shape split and Dootsie came running through the snow and suddenly I gasped and tears came because I knew who the remaining huddled shape must be. I ran to meet Dootsie and scooped her up and ran to the sled. Somewhere in the bundle of blankets two moonlit eyes peeped out. "Is that you in there, Betty Lou?" I said.

Came a tiny, trembly voice and a frosty puff: "Yes."

"Did Dootsie barge into your house this morning and drag you out of bed and make you come here?"

"Yes."

Dootsie piped: "I did! I did!"

"Do you wish you were back in your house?"

"Yes."

"Do you feel unsafe?"

"Yes."

Dootsie stuck her face into the bundle. I heard her muffled

voice: "Don't worry, Betty Lou. We won't let anything happen to you."

"Pull her there," I said to Mr. and Mrs. Pringle, pointing to the two-sided tent. "Give her the best seat."

As they pulled the sled away, other figures were appearing at the edge of the field, wading through the snow:

Alvina and her little brother, Thomas, and their parents.

Arnold and Tom and Arnold's mother, Rita. Tom was in Arnold's coat pocket. I lifted the flap of my coat pocket to introduce Cinnamon to Tom, and next thing I knew Cinnamon was joining Tom in Arnold's pocket. Arnold was tickled, so I let them be.

Ike the bike-and-mower man.

My porch light neighbors along Rapps Dam Road.

The reporter from the *Morning Lenape*.

A gaggle of boys, Alvina's tormentors, including the blond-haired one she beat up at the Dogwood Festival and whose picture hangs on her bedroom door.

The Honeybees.

Margie.

Charlie.

And then a couple that had me stumped. Even from a distance I could tell they were old. They clung to each other as they made their way slowly through the snow. When I saw their faces I remembered them from somewhere—and then I knew. The Huffelmeyers of the Friday milk route: 1 qt buttermk, 1 qt choc. They were much younger in most of the pictures in the dining room. It was as if they had walked out of a family album. They saw me and came right up. I was looking down on both of them. Mr. Huffelmeyer said, "Is this your idea?"

"It is," I said. "I'm the Solstice girl. I'm the milk girl too. My father drives the dairy truck." I pointed at them. "Fridays. Two-fourteen White Horse Road. One buttermilk, one chocolate."

"Glory be," said Mrs. Huffelmeyer.

"Can I ask you something?" I said. "I've been wondering for months."

Mr. Huffelmeyer nodded. "Shoot."

"Who gets the buttermilk and who gets the chocolate?"

They laughed, harder than I might have thought folks their age could without breaking into pieces. "Both of us," said Mrs. Huffelmeyer. "We mix them. It's our big treat." She twirled her finger in the air. "Whoopee."

"We thank you for the good service," said her husband. "And your father."

"No," I said, "thank *you*. For letting us into your home. Thank you for trusting us."

I held out my hand to shake, but they were having none of it. Only long, hard hugs would do. I ushered them to a spot next to Betty Lou.

I kept looking out for Perry. Why wasn't he showing up? The crowd was getting bigger by the minute. My father was right—they were already spilling out of the tent's dimensions. Had I said something to offend him when we met on the street a week ago? Was he miffed over my reaction to

Dootsie's tattoo? Did he give up on girls who won't become Honeybees?

The sky was pearly gray in the east when I saw the flashing lights of the police car. I met the policeman halfway across the field.

"You in charge?" he said.

"I guess so," I said.

He looked over my shoulder at the crowd. "What's going on?"

"Winter Solstice," I said. "We're here to watch the sunrise."

He looked at me.

Behind me, Margie's voice: "Hey, Mike."

The policeman nodded. "Margie."

"Problem?"

"Public gathering? Permit?"

Margie laughed. "This is not a demonstration. Nobody's disturbing the peace. We're here to watch a sunbeam, Mike. A *sunbeam*."

She took his arm and led him toward his car. "Let's turn those lights off and you can join us." And that was that with the law.

And then I saw Perry—Perry and tiny blue-blanketed Clarissa in his arms and their mother, Neva. I looked at the eastern sky. Sun mist drifted above the treetops. "Hurry!" I called. "You're almost late." I practically dragged them along. I put them up front, next to the Huffelmeyers.

Still they kept coming, many of them faces I did not

recognize. All the while Dootsie and Alvina were handing out yellow sunburst buttons. We were well beyond the invited number now, the number of buttons I had told them to make, yet the buttons kept coming. I thought of the miracle of the fishes. I found out later that Alvina had bought more yellow foam sheets and pins on her own and had kept making buttons. "You're so dumb," she said. "I knew it was gonna be mobbed."

It was time. I walked through the trampled snow to the people. I stood at the front tent panel. Everyone was looking at me and the panel with the round hole and the eastern sky beyond. I moved forward toward the back panel. The crowd gave way. I couldn't believe so many had come. I had offered no explanation or persuasion on the invitations. I assumed that, except for Perry and Archie and a few others, most of them knew little if anything of the astronomical realities that called us to this place at this time. Yet here they were. And I must tell you that others were there too: the Lenape maiden and the boy she fell for and Grace, Charlie's Grace, and many more, many more than a camera could ever see. So many, and I couldn't have said why.

I stood before the back panel. Some were still facing away, eastward. "Look this way," I said. "The hole will squeeze the first light of winter into a beam that will land"—I took a deep breath and pointed—"here."

Then I stepped aside—and that was all I did. I had decided the night before, after talking with Archie, that there would be no performance, no ceremony. I would not wear special clothes. I would not sing. I would not dance. I had torn up the poem I had written, left the bittersweet wreath and ukulele at home. I would not dress the dog. I would let nature speak for itself.

When I think back on it, I'm not sure which was the highlight for me—the sunrise itself or the moments before. I stood to one side, next to Archie, Betty Lou's sled in front of me. I would never have guessed that so many people could be so silent. It was more than the absence of sound. It was a presence. An expectation. A reverence. All of us staring at the blank tent wall, the black curtain that would not un-cover the show but would become the show itself, staring, waiting, as pure a waiting as I've ever known. I never had the sense that it arrived—it was simply *not there*, and then it was *there*: a long thin stem of light the width of Dootsie's lit-tle wrist, a thin golden gift from the sun come 93 million miles to mark a perfect golden circle on the Blackbone panel. Gasps erupted behind me. The circle blurred as tears filled my eyes. Someone sobbed, "Oh my." Someone cried softly, "Beautiful!" Many of us could have reached out and touched the golden stem. No one did.

I felt a tug. It was Betty Lou. She was reaching back, grabbing my hand, pulling me. I leaned forward. She whis-pered: "Thank you." Archie held my other hand.

Someone was moving on the other side of the golden stem. It was Perry. He took a sideways step and held out his new baby sister until her blue blanket sliced the light, intercepting the beam. He moved her until the sunburst button on her blanket fell in line with the sunbeam's circle, and when they came together they were a perfect match. The baby, wide-eyed at the crowd, seemed to know it was a unique moment. Perry held her like that briefly, looked across at me and smiled and nodded, and took her back to his place.

The beam began to dissipate then, as the sun cleared the horizon and flooded the world with light. Still the people stayed, watching as the golden circle frayed and dissolved across the Blackbone. It reminded me of a movie that is so good the audience just sits there staring at the rolling credits after the lights go on. Suddenly the simple phrase "another day" had new meaning.

In time the people began to stir and head back to their cars and bicycles. There was some whispering among them, but not much. Many were wiping their eyes. Mrs. Huffelmeyer hugged me. So did Charlie, and others. Alvina and Dootsie bickered over the leftover buttons. I spotted Alvina across the snowfield. She was walking behind the blond-haired boy. She reached out. . . . *Oh no!* I thought . . . and then I smiled, because she didn't hit him, she merely touched his shoulder and veered away. She was counting coup. The boy turned to look after her but I couldn't see the expression on his face.

Dootsie called, "Stargirl, look!" She was holding baby Clarissa. Perry looked a bit nervous, but Neva was smiling easily as she held on to Ike's arm. And then Dootsie was calling, "Your turn!" and running for me. "Stay!" I called. Perry lurched, but I got there first and took the baby. I have never seen a face as filled with gratitude as Perry's at that moment. I talked with Clarissa and we got to know each other a little and agreed to meet again soon. And then Perry and his family left and Arnold's mother, Rita, came by to return Cinnamon, and when I turned around again everyone was gone but Archie and my parents and Dootsie.

Nothing is more forlorn, more useless, than an expired calendar. My father was pulling up tent rope stakes, and my mother was coming at me with both arms out, saying, "I'm so proud of you!" She threw her arms around me and I lost it. I burst into tears. I was surprised. I hadn't felt it coming. I went on and on. Curiously, no one tried to stop me. I left my mother and walked off by myself into the snowfield, crying away. I didn't get far before a little hand slipped into mine. I'm sure Dootsie was too young to understand what was going on—heck, *I* was too young—and yet I know that she and I were somehow touching the same thing. She didn't say a word, just walked slowly through the snow with me toward the horizon in the west, where the sun would later bring this day to a close. When we stopped and turned back, the Blackbone sheets were down and the last of the tent poles was falling.

December 24

Archie went home today. He didn't want Señor Saguaro to be alone for Christmas.

Yesterday we talked late into the night. Somewhere around his third pipe bowl of cherry tobacco he said, "Do you know why you cried the other day?"

"Yes and no," I said.

"Many reasons, yes?"

"Yes."

"Hard to give a name to."

"Yes."

"But one reason—"

"Yes."

"—does have a name."

I looked at him. "Yes."

He pulled a small folded envelope from his shirt pocket. "He asked me to give this to you. He knew about your Solstice, from me and your friend Dori Dilson. He said to give it to you after it was over. He didn't want to distract you. Maybe that was a mistake, but"—he shrugged—"I just do what I'm told." He handed me the envelope.

I was about to rip it open, then feared I might rip the contents too. I got a steak knife from the drawer. I didn't trust myself. I gave the knife and envelope to Archie. "You open it. Be careful."

He slit open the envelope and returned it to me. My hands were shaking. It was a single piece of paper, white, small, folded in quarters, the way a little kid folds a letter. Fold by fold I opened it. There was one word, in bold royal blue marker ink, all capital letters:

YES

My heart took flight. You heard me, didn't you, dear, dear Leo? All those sunrise mornings when I sat on Calendar Hill with my eyes closed, when I turned from the sunrise to face the west, sending you my message, my question:

Will we ever meet again?

And you received it—I knew you would, I *knew* it, I *knew* it—and now you've answered.

"Oh no, not again," Archie was saying, but he was being playful because he could see that my tears were happy ones this time. I laughed and told him all about it as Cinnamon nibbled around the edges of YES.

January 2

Christmas and New Year's were both kind of lost on me this time around. Wonder why.

I've been daydreaming a lot lately, taking long walks, bike rides. I went to Calendar Hill for one last time. It looks so ordinary now, just another field on another hill. I stood in the middle, where the croquet stake had been. I tried to conjure the magic of that morning, but I could not. But I did feel something else, a lingering presence of the people who had been there. And a sudden swelling of affection for them. I see them wearing their sunburst buttons around town. Margie has had some made and gives one to each customer who orders a dozen donuts.

Nothing has really changed, and yet in some hard-to-explain way, everything has. Dootsie begs me five times a day to let her saw me in half. She got a magic kit for Christmas. Alvina has turned twelve. I gave her a doll for her birthday. My mother made two outfits for it: a gown and karate jamas. Arnold shuffles forth daily, waiting to be found. Charlie sits in his red and yellow scarf and talks to Grace.

For the first week after Solstice, Betty Lou came outside only if someone pulled her in a sled or wagon. On New Year's Day Dootsie and I each took a hand and walked her around the block. This morning she called me, thrilled: "I just walked to the mailbox! By myself!" Perry pushes his new baby sister around town, and sometimes I do too. I've become chief babysitter. I am referred to as Aunt Stargirl. Clarissa's second home has already become Margie's, where Neva will begin working again next week.

Oh yes—Cinnamon. I got a call from Arnold's mother, Rita. It seems that Tom, despite the name, is pregnant. Apparently Arnold has a fertile coat pocket. Cinnamon is going to be a daddy!

And my happy wagon is holding steady at seventeen pebbles.

And so the days pass, twelve of them since the sun began its journey back to summer. Ordinary days, ordinary creatures. Ordinary, usual, everyday life—and yet it all seems so special now, the commonest gestures flecked with glitter, as if a sparkle from the golden beam clung to every person who went down from Calendar Hill that morning.

As I stood that final time on the hill, I decided that—yes—I will mail this world's longest letter to you. I know now that you too were there that morning, as surely as the Lenape maiden and Charlie's Grace were there. Your answer has been a new sunrise for me, my own personal Solstice, the dawn of a season that I will, as Betty Lou would say, inhabit one day at a time. I will sail into the future on mystery's wings and I will not look back. Oh yes, I do love Arnold, but I have been too much like him. We Arnolds, our hearts yearn backward. We long to be found, hoping our searchers have not given up and gone home. But I no longer hope to be found, Leo. Do not follow me! Let's just be fabulously where we are and who we are. You be you and I'll be me, today and today and today, and let's trust the future to tomorrow. Let the stars keep track of us. Let us ride our own orbits and trust that they will meet. May our reunion be not a finding but a sweet collision of destinies!

Love and Love and Love Again,

JERRY SPINELLI is the author of many books for young readers, including *Stargirl; Milkweed; Crash; Maniac Magee*, winner of the Newbery Medal; *Wringer*, winner of a Newbery Honor; *Eggs*; and *Knots in My Yo-yo String*, his autobiography. A graduate of Gettysburg College, he lives in Pennsylvania with his wife, poet and author Eileen Spinelli.